W.

KU-489-930

FAR LIES THE SHORE

Calanara was an island with a secret. What caused the rift between Tansy's mother and her grandfather? And why was the hostile Mark Harmon opposed to her plans for Whitton Lodge Nurseries? Probing past events helped Tansy to find solutions to the problems of the present, only to discover that there was no place for her on the island. Yet something about Calanara called to her and the longer she stayed, the harder it became to leave . . .

MARIAN HIPWELL

FAR LIES
THE SHORE

Complete and Unabridged

LINFORD
Leicester

First published in Great Britain in 1991 by
Robert Hale Limited
London

First Linford Edition
published 2006
by arrangement with
Robert Hale Limited
London

British Library CIP Data

Hipwell, Marian
Far lies the shore.—Large print ed.—
Linford romance library
1. Love stories
2. Large type books
I. Title
823.9'14 [F]

ISBN 1–84617–340–X

Published by
F. A. Thorpe (Publishing)
Anstey, Leicestershire

Set by Words & Graphics Ltd.
Anstey, Leicestershire
Printed and bound in Great Britain by
T. J. International Ltd., Padstow, Cornwall

This book is printed on acid-free paper

1

'Miss Forrester? Welcome to Calanara.'

The voice was cool, with hardly a hint of warmth, despite the greeting. The grey eyes regarding Tansy registered a disapproval their owner was powerless to hide. Tansy's mouth tightened. She had not left her job in the middle of an important negotiation and endured an uncomfortable few hours on the ferry ploughing between the mainland and this quaintly named island to be faced with disapproval from a stranger, particularly one whom she suspected was now in her employment.

'I'm Mark Harmon.'

His terse introduction of himself confirmed her suspicions. She had picked out his tall figure from the others waiting for the ferry to dock, guessing he was her late grandfather's general manager; the man, according to the solicitors dealing with Benson Whitton's estate, who had been running the nurseries single-handed over the last few weeks.

'This is your luggage? Just one small piece?' He gestured towards the suitcase by Tansy's side and she nodded.

'Yes. I won't be staying long.' She spoke abstractedly, her mind already busy with the need to find a telephone and contact her office. They weren't that far from the mainland, yet judging from first impressions, she might as well be at the other end of the world for all the hope she had of keeping in touch with things.

'Oh, yes.' His eyes held a touch of irony as he caught her gaze. 'You're just here to sell up, aren't you?'

'That's right.' Irritated by the barely concealed scorn in his tone, Tansy spoke coolly. Her plans for the business she had inherited so unexpectedly were no concern of his. Even now, some time after the event, it seemed strange to her that she had been left a thriving plant nursery business by a grandfather she had never met and whom she had presumed was unaware of her existence.

'I thought we might have seen you at the funeral.' There was no doubting the reproof in his tone, and she answered defensively.

'I was out of town on business at the time of my grandfather's death. The funeral had already taken place by the time the solicitors managed to contact me.' She was uncomfortably aware of his scrutiny. He was sceptical of her explanation, that was obvious. And, perhaps, wondering what the future held in store, now that Benson Whitton was dead. She could understand his feelings. Her grandfather, by all accounts, had left the running of the nurseries to his general manager, particularly in the last months of his life, and Mark Harmon would have expected things to go on in the same way under her ownership. With the business taken over by Paul Tregarth of Tregarth Leisure Industries as she hoped, it would be a different matter altogether.

Her decision to sell had seemed to take Mark Harmon by surprise when she had mentioned it briefly over the telephone a few days ago. His anger had been evident immediately in the sudden curtness of his tone. He had, she recalled, only just succeeded in maintaining the level of politeness demanded by his position as her employee.

'How long will you be staying?' he asked, as they made their way to a parked Land Rover.

'Oh — ' Tansy spoke vaguely. 'I've taken a couple of weeks' leave but I want to get back as quickly as I can. I have an important account on my hands at the moment and I can't afford to be away from the office for long.'

'Advertising, isn't it?' He glanced briefly at her. 'Pretty high-powered stuff. I hope you don't find Calanara too dull.'

They were moving away now and Tansy glanced curiously through the window as the vehicle edged its way out of the harbour and in the direction of a country lane, giving Tansy her first glimpse of the place. The mist which had obscured the island's outline from her view whilst on the ferry had lifted, to reveal soft, rolling downs stretching away into the distance. To the west, her gaze met the shimmering silhouette of purple-topped hills, whilst to the east, the sea sparkled like a silver cloth in the pale afternoon light.

'I'd forgotten; this is your first visit, isn't it?' Though he had obviously made an effort to keep his tone non-committal, Tansy still detected the implied criticism.

'My grandfather and I weren't exactly on visiting terms,' she informed him drily. 'As I'm sure you know.'

'Benson didn't discuss his personal affairs with me.' He spoke coolly. 'Though I do know some of the story, as it happens. My mother and yours were good friends, a long time ago. In fact, our families have been involved for years.'

'Oh?' Tansy eyed him curiously. It occurred to her that he probably knew more about the breach between her mother and her grandfather than she did herself. Her mother had always been unwilling to discuss the past, and knowing how painful the memories were, Tansy had seldom pressed matters. Knowing what Benson Whitton had done to her parents' marriage had been enough . . . She eyed the stern profile of the man beside her, guessing shrewdly that he was not enjoying the prospect of her company over the next few days, entailing as it did the necessity of his playing host to a woman for whom Whitton Lodge Nurseries held no interest whatsoever.

Aware of the lengthening silence between them, she made an effort at conversation.

'Presumably this is a busy time for the nurseries?'

'That's right.' His tone thawed somewhat, enthusiasm creeping into it. 'Our main concern at the moment is the flower show later this year. And now that the summer annuals are in hand, we're already well into the autumn trade.' He eyed her speculatively. 'It's a pity you won't be here for the flower show. I'm sure you'd enjoy it.'

'A pity,' Tansy agreed pleasantly.

'Have you any prospective buyers in mind for the place yet, since you're determined to sell it?' He spoke quickly, as if reluctant to discuss the matter. 'That's if you don't mind my asking?' he added.

'Of course not; it concerns you, after all. There have been some negotiations but nothing definite yet.'

Tansy spoke warily, choosing her words with care. Though nothing specific had been agreed in the brief conversation she'd had with Paul Tregarth, she had been left with the feeling that his plans for Whitton Lodge Nurseries did not include its continuing along the present lines. The owner of a large piece of land adjoining the nurseries, it seemed likely that Tregarth's intentions would be to incorporate the nursery land with his own in some way, though he had assured her that there would be no redundancies among the nursery staff. Noting the enthusiasm in Mark Harmon's voice when talking about the work of the nurseries a few moments ago, she had a feeling that Tregarth's plans for the place would not meet with his approval.

They had turned now, heading into the open countryside, their progress slowing as the Landrover negotiated the uneven track.

'The nurseries are over there; you can just about see them.' Mark Harmon gestured into the distance and, following his pointing finger, Tansy made out the outline of buildings some miles ahead. Sun reflected on rows of greenhouses, dazzling her, and she put a hand to her eyes, shading her view.

'The main greenhouse is at the front.' Pride had crept into his voice. 'You can't see the research unit from here, but over there — ' he gestured to the left, ' — that's the house. Whitton Lodge.'

Tansy leaned forward, eager for a better view. As they drew closer, her first impressions were that it was all somewhat larger than she had expected.

'Research unit?' She eyed Mark Harmon enquiringly.

'Yes; we try out new strains and seeding methods,' he informed her. 'Your grandfather was keen on trying new ideas.'

Tansy stifled a sigh. It seemed to her, in the short time she had known this man, that he took every opportunity which presented itself to extol her grandfather's and the nurseries' virtues, stressing the fact that she was an outsider, with little knowledge of how things worked in their particular field, and even less intention of finding out. The sooner she and Paul Tregarth brought their negotiations to a satisfactory conclusion the better, if this was the way things were going to be.

The track had widened now into

some semblance of a road as they approached the entrance to the nurseries, and Tansy had her first clear view of them. The house rising sharply some distance away from the cluster of glass buildings was obviously Whitton Lodge. From this distance, it looked large and imposing, though still in keeping with the character of the surrounding area. The ground-floor window had an unhindered view of the nurseries and Tansy had a momentary picture in her mind's eye of the old man, her grandfather, keeping a firm visual control over everything. Not for the first time, she wondered what he had been like, this man who had disapproved of his only daughter's choice of husband so much he had deliberately done all he could to wreck the marriage, causing a breach between his daughter and himself that time had never healed. A man like that would not have found it easy to humble himself and ask for forgiveness, and his daughter had made no move towards reconciliation. As she had done many times before, Tansy wondered now if she could have done more to bring the two of them together, yet her tentative attempts at broaching the subject to her mother had met with resounding failure. And now Benson Whitton was dead and it was too late.

The Land Rover had passed the greenhouse now, heading away from them and in the direction of the house, coming to a stop alongside the huge oak door. Tansy eyed the house with interest.

'So this is where my grandfather lived,' she murmured.

In the act of leaving the vehicle, Mark Harmon paused and nodded, his eyes following hers towards the house.

'He was pretty lonely here during the last years, though we did our best,' he said quietly after a moment.

Tansy was aware of a flicker of irritation. Why did he persist in trying to make her feel guilty about what he apparently saw as her neglect of her grandfather?

11

'Yes; from what I've heard of him, he wouldn't make friends easily,' she murmured coolly.

'He was proud and stubborn, admittedly,' Mark responded. 'But he could be a good friend to those who gave him their loyalty.'

Was that another rebuke for her, Tansy wondered?

'That's where my mother and I live.' He pointed down the lane in the direction of a neat, white-walled cottage some way beyond the main nursery buildings. 'Gatehouse Cottage. It takes its name from the fact that this place once housed the lord of the island; you can see the castle ruins in the distance. Gatehouse Cottage was where the sentries were housed, though we have modernised it somewhat.' His tone was wry. 'My mother acted as your grandfather's housekeeper and still keeps things tidy. She's been in the Lodge this morning, sorting things out for you, so I gather.' As he spoke, he was moving briskly towards the front door of Whitton Lodge, taking a key from his pocket. 'She's put you in the small bedroom at the back, I understand,' he went on. 'It's warmer there, with a good view over the hills.'

Opening the door, he stood aside for Tansy to enter, then followed her in, waiting as she looked around her. Pleasantly furnished, the house was airier than its sombre exterior suggested, with bright curtains at the windows lending a homely touch to the obviously masculine atmosphere. Plant arrangements relieved the gloom and the faint smell of lavender had her nostrils twitching appreciatively. She became aware then that Mark Harmon was obviously expecting some sort of comment from her.

'Everything's very nice,' she said quickly. Crossing to a small table further down the hallway, she picked up the bowl of white and silver flowers standing on it and breathed in their fragrance.

'Lovely,' she murmured. 'Please thank

your mother for making everything so pleasant.'

Mark Harmon's eyes flickered and Tansy had the impression she had annoyed him. The remark, she realised now, sounded formal and facetious, yet she had not meant it to sound that way.

'I'll pass on your message,' he said stiffly. 'And I'll leave you now to settle in. If there's anything you need, you can get in touch with us at the cottage easily enough.' He gestured towards two telephones on the table. 'One's a direct line outside and the other an internal, coming through to us. The freezer's stocked up, if you're hungry.' He hesitated. 'My mother asked me to invite you to dinner tonight, but if you'd rather have a quiet evening on your own — '

'Oh, I'd love to come,' Tansy assured him.

An indefinable expression flitted across his face and she guessed he'd expected — hoped, even — that she would refuse. Nor was she particularly keen to spend an evening in his company, yet it would have been churlish to have refused his mother's invitation.

'I'll be on my way then.' He moved towards the door. 'Around eight o'clock?'

'Whenever it's convenient for you,' Tansy responded.

'Fine.' A brief smile touched his face, making it look less stern. Fleetingly, she compared him with David Firth, her office colleague and frequent escort; the man, in fact, who was handling her accounts for her whilst she was on the island. There was a certain similarity between the two men, she couldn't help thinking. They both had the same dedication to their work and lack of patience with people who did not feel the same way. Yet, whereas David possessed an easy charm which drew people to him instantly, there was a reserve about this man which would, she felt, be difficult to pierce, even if his opinion of her were not so low. Having spent most of his life on the island, too, he would view what he saw as her city sophistication with distrust.

'Heather Parker, my assistant, will be dining with us,' he said unexpectedly. 'So you'll have a chance to meet one member of staff, at least.'

'Good.' Tansy spoke sincerely, yet she couldn't help wondering if the other woman's invitation was merely for the safe of introducing her or if there was another purpose behind it. Did he think, for instance, that by mustering as much support as he could, he would be able to force her in the direction in which he wanted her to go? She didn't know. But one thing she was sure of. She did not intend to be bullied by him or anyone else on this island . . .

After he had left, she spent some time wandering around the house. There were several bedrooms and a surprisingly modern bathroom which she lost no time in using, luxuriating in a sweetly scented bath. She was about to step outside and explore the garden some time later when she became aware of the telephone ringing and hurried to answer it.

'Miss Forrester? Paul Tregarth here. I'm so glad I caught you.' The voice was brisk.

'Oh, Mr Tregarth — hello! How are you?' Tansy responded.

'I'm well, thanks. Look — ' He was obviously eager to cut the preliminaries short. 'I was hoping to arrange a meeting between us very soon, but something's come up. I've some urgent business overseas which won't wait.'

'Oh.' Tansy couldn't hide her dismay. She was as keen to get negotiations started as he was.

'I'm really sorry we can't get together yet.' He spoke regretfully. 'But I should be back in a day or two, if things go according to plan. Can you hang on?'

'Well — ' Tansy hesitated. 'How long?' She hadn't planned to stay any longer than was absolutely necessary.

'Please, bear with me,' he appealed. 'I'll get back to you as quickly as I can.

Or I could contact your solicitors in the city.'

'No.' Caution held her back, despite her eagerness to resolve things. She had come here with the idea of settling things personally whilst on the island. The employees of Whitton Lodge Nurseries must hear the news of the impending take-over from her, not from some other source. 'I'll wait for your return,' she added.

'All right. I'll be in touch.' The line clicked and he was gone. Replacing the receiver, Tansy frowned. This was going to take longer than she had anticipated . . . Glancing at her watch, she remembered that she had meant to telephone David Firth, yet it was too late to catch him at the office. There was no answer when she rang his flat; he was obviously out for the evening. For a moment she felt wistful, wishing she were with him instead of on this small island, preparing to dine with a man who had hardly troubled to hide his feelings of hostility towards her. She dressed with care later, having no wish to confirm Mark Harmon's already formed view of her, yet needing the reassurance of knowing she looked her best. She was, after all, the owner of Whitton Lodge Nurseries, even if only temporarily; a fact she felt Mark Harmon needed to have made clear to him. Throwing a wrap around her shoulders, she left the house and set off for Gatehouse Cottage. It was larger than it had appeared when viewed from the Lodge, she saw as she drew nearer. Bright and informal where the Lodge was imposing, it had a friendly, welcoming air about it, helped along by the riot of colour from the flowers which bordered the small front garden. As she approached the front door, it opened and an elderly woman advanced towards her, smiling.

'Miss Forrester! I'm so pleased you decided to come.' There was no doubting the sincerity of the woman's greeting as she walked towards Tansy, her hands outstretched in a welcoming gesture. 'I'm Laura Harmon, Mark's mother,' she introduced herself. There was none of her son's stiffness of manner about her and the smile she was bestowing on Tansy was filled with warmth. Tansy was immediately drawn to her.

'Thank you for inviting me,' she said impulsively.

As the older woman drew her into the hallway, the murmur of voices could be heard; Mark Harmon's deeper tones mingling with other, lighter ones.

'You're the image of your grandfather; did you know?' Laura Harmon was eyeing her appraisingly.

'We never met,' Tansy explained.

'Oh, well.' The older woman spoke gently. 'You're here now.'

Hearing her, Tansy was uneasily aware of the feeling that people here expected her to take what they saw as her rightful place at Whitton Lodge, now that she had come to the island. It was one thing to tell herself that Mark Harmon would have to abide by her decision; explaining the position to this sweet-faced woman would be quite another. There was no time for further introspection. Mark Harmon was approaching her now, his eyes filled with just the correct amount of formal welcome as they rested on her.

'Miss Forrester. You found us then?' he murmured.

Laura Harmon gave him a reproachful glance. 'I told you to collect Miss Forrester from the Lodge,' she chided.

'Can't we be a little less formal?' Tansy asked. 'My name's Tansy.'

'Tansy. How lovely!' Laura Harmon's voice was approving. 'Your mother's choice, I imagine. She always loved those flowers. They grow here in profusion.'

And yet she never came back to see them, Tansy couldn't help thinking. The rift between Benson Whitton and his daughter had been deep enough to transcend all other issues.

'She emigrated, I heard,' Laura commented.

'Yes; a year ago. She and Peter — her husband — are very happy,' Tansy told her. 'Mr Harmon was telling me — '

'Mark, please, since you prefer less formality,' he said.

Tansy caught his eye, unaccountably irritated by his interruption. If he preferred things to continue on an employer/employee basis, that was fine by her. His gaze was challenging and she realized once more that if she had hoped to get things over with smoothly, she had reckoned without him.

'Very well.' Her voice was cool. Turning back to Laura Harmon, she continued. 'Mark tells me you were a good friend of my mother's years ago. She never talked about her early days on the island. In fact, I was well into my teens before I knew my grandfather was still alive.'

'That's right.' Laura Harmon smiled reflectively. 'Though we lost touch years ago. Come and meet Heather.' She drew Tansy towards the lounge now. 'She's a relative of yours; did you know?

Her parents were cousins of your grandfather's.'

'Really?' Tansy eyed her in surprise. 'I'd no idea.' Entering the room, she caught sight of the woman standing by the window. Around Tansy's own age, she smiled nervously as they approached her.

'Hello.' Tansy spoke warmly, trying to put the other woman at her ease. 'We're sort of cousins, I hear.'

'That's right.' Despite her friendly response, the other woman's eyes held a guarded look which Tansy couldn't fail to be aware of.

'Drink?' Mark Harmon was eyeing Tansy enquiringly and she accepted. 'The usual for you, Heather?' he added.

'Yes please, Mark.'

Watching, Tansy was aware of an easy intimacy between the two of them which she felt went beyond the usual professional working relationship. It would be no great surprise to her to find she had judged the situation correctly. On first acquaintance, Heather

Parker seemed to be the perfect choice for Mark Harmon. Part of the Whitton circle, an islander like himself, with the same upbringing and outlook, she already had enough in common with him before taking into account their shared interest in Whitton Lodge Nurseries. Heather Parker would fit perfectly into Mark Harmon's life, she felt.

The atmosphere relaxed somewhat as they dined later. Mark had contrived to seat himself beside Heather and across from Tansy, so that she was even more aware of the feeling of their being united against her, ready to oppose anything which they felt might threaten their way of life.

'I'm sure Tansy will want to look around the nurseries tomorrow, Mark.' Laura looked up from pouring coffee later.

'Are you?' There was something in Mark's voice which had Tansy glancing quickly at him. He held her gaze broodingly, his fingers twisting the stem of the wineglass he was holding; almost,

Tansy thought, as if he were daring her to speak up and reveal her plans for the nurseries. And it was time she did. It wasn't fair to hold back any longer, particularly whilst accepting their hospitality. Anger at his obvious attempt to force the issue into the open mingled with sudden uneasiness. She couldn't pretend to herself that these people would welcome her intention of selling to Tregarth, yet what could she do? Couldn't they see that it was in everyone's interests that she sold to someone who was prepared to invest time and money in the business? In the hands of an uncaring owner, it could only go one way . . . Why couldn't they understand that she had no wish to be involved with anything connected with Benson Whitton, after the way he had treated her parents?

Looking round, she saw the bowl of flowers on the coffee-table, their silvery white petals recalling the ones she had noticed at the Lodge. Picking them up, she caught their fragrance.

'Lovely, aren't they?' Laura asked, smiling. 'The island's very own wild flower. They grow nowhere else in the world, so far as we know.' Taking the bowl from Tansy, she stroked the feathery petals gently. 'We call them Merlin's Tears.'

'What an unusual name!' Tansy's curiosity vied with relief at the turn the conversation had taken; postponing, if only for a few minutes, the announcement she knew she would have to make concerning the nurseries.

'There's a legend connected with these flowers,' Laura murmured. 'According to it, Merlin the Wizard spent his last days here. In fact, there's a cavern on the hillside, a local beauty spot known as Merlin's Cavern. The story goes that he was imprisoned there. He fell in love but the lady didn't return his feelings, particularly when she left Camelot and he insisted on following her.' She smiled briefly. 'It had been foretold to him that he would be imprisoned in a cavern in that area. She persuaded him to show her the cavern, even got him to roll back the stone guarding the entrance, and go inside. Then she used her magic to roll back the stone and he was imprisoned there.'

'How sad,' Tansy murmured.

'The legend has it that when he realized the extent of her treachery, he wept bitterly.' Mark Harmon took up the story. 'The tears found their way underneath the stone and out into the open, rolling down the hillside. Soon afterwards, so the story goes, these tiny flowers appeared and have grown there ever since. They came to be known as Merlin's Tears and all attempts to cultivate them or get them to grow elsewhere have failed.'

'Almost as if they were Merlin's gift to the island,' Laura murmured. 'And he wanted the people here to keep them to perpetuate his memory.'

'You're a romantic, mother!' Mark gave her an affectionate look. 'It's more likely he wanted to perpetuate the memory of a woman's treachery.' The words, innocent in themselves, seemed to Tansy's ears barbed and heavy with a meaning directed towards herself. She forced herself to respond coolly.

'That wouldn't be an allusion of some sort to me, would it?'

'Are you going to tell us Paul Tregarth's sudden appearance on the island after a lengthy absence, at the same time as your own arrival, is a coincidence?' he countered. Beside her, Tansy heard Laura's sharp intake of breath and she turned, giving her an apologetic look.

'I'd hoped to wait until we had finished our coffee at least, before talking business,' she said. 'The fact is, Paul Tregarth has expressed an interest in acquiring the nurseries — '

'So I was right!' Mark interrupted softly.

Tansy eyed him spiritedly. 'I made no secret of the fact that I was interested in selling,' she pointed out.

'But to *him*?' The last word was spoken savagely. 'You intend to hand

28

over the nurseries to a man who wants to bulldoze them in order to turn them into a golf-course for his rich clients? You *are* aware that's what he plans for us, I take it?' Despite his deceptively quiet tone, his face was white now with anger.

'How can you know that?' Tansy asked. 'It's true he has plans for — '

'Oh, he has plans, all right!' Mark Harmon's laugh made an incongruous sound in the quiet room. 'And what of our employees, Miss Forrester, your grandfather's employees who served him loyally over the years? Have you no thought for them?'

'Mr Tregarth assures me there will be jobs for everyone,' Tansy insisted.

'As what?' he demanded. 'Greenkeepers, servants to pick up behind the people who patronize his exorbitantly priced health farm? Is that what they can look forward to, people with skills and years of experience in this trade? People who stood behind your grandfather — '

'Mr Harmon!' Despite the coolness

of her voice, Tansy was shaking with anger. Standing up, she faced him. 'Let's get something clear. My grandfather is dead. I am now the owner of Whitton Lodge Nurseries, and I will make the decisions regarding its future.'

Struggling impotently to control his anger, Mark looked at his mother. 'Does she still remind you of Benson Whitton?' he grated.

'As a matter of fact, she does!' Laura surprised them all by saying. 'He stood up for whatever he felt was right. And he allowed no one to tell him what to do! Now, why don't we all calm down and talk quietly about this?'

'Why?' Mark made a dismissive gesture. 'It's probably all signed and sealed. We've been working here, keeping the nurseries going as a viable concern, so that Tregarth can turn them into clubrooms! As for the greenhouses and research unit, they'll be razed to the ground. They wouldn't be much use to him.' He eyed Tansy bitterly. 'All the years of research and experimenting gone, so that you can go back to the mainland with a nicely swollen bank account, an insurance for your old age; something Benson Whitton's employees can't look forward to, under Tregarth's control! As for his offer of jobs, do you think they would take them? Do you think *I* would take a job with Tregarth, even if one were offered to me — which I doubt!' He clenched his fists by his sides. 'After years of trying to harass Benson Whitton into selling out, all Tregarth had to do, once he knew Benson was ill, was sit it out until you came along to hand the business over to him, lock, stock and barrel!'

'That's not quite the situation!' Tansy strove for calmness. 'All we've done so far is talk. There's no way I'd see Tregarth harm the nursery employees! Take-overs happen all the time, not always to the detriment of the business being taken over — '

'Stop pretending you care about your grandfather's employees!' He made no effort to hide his scorn now. 'All you

31

care about is getting out of here — '

'That part's right!' Tansy was goaded into saying. 'And if you're an indication of the rest of the island population, the sooner I leave, the better!'

'I'm glad you're honest about that, at any rate!' His voice was filled with satisfaction.

'What do you expect me to do?' Tansy looked round them all in sudden helplessness. 'I work in advertising. I'm highly trained and I love my job; I don't want to change direction — '

'You could leave things the way they are, with me in charge!' Mark Harmon grated. 'Instead of selling the place!'

'And that's what this is all about, isn't it?' Tansy eyed him shrewdly. 'You want things to stay as they are, with you running the place, you being the boss!'

Catching sight of Heather Parker's strained expression over Mark's shoulder, Tansy drew in her breath, as a thought occurred to her. Mark Harmon and Heather — a distant cousin of Benson Whitton's — were on friendly terms; she had seen that for herself. Had Mark hoped to get his hands on this business, which obviously meant so much to him, by marrying Heather? Had he hoped Benson Whitton would leave the nurseries to Heather? It was possible he hadn't even been aware of Tansy's existence until recently. If so, what a blow it must have been for him to have his plans thwarted in this way! And if he had entertained a hope that she might allow herself to be manipulated in the direction in which he wanted things to go, it must have soon become apparent to him that it was a forlorn hope. She wasn't Heather Parker. She would not be told what to do by this man.

His unjustified — in her eyes — hostility only served to strengthen her determination now. This inheritance, which she had neither sought nor wanted, would not be allowed to interfere with her life. Benson Whitton had ruined her mother's life, because she had gone against his wishes. Neither he, nor his business, would be allowed to do that to her own life. The deal with Tregarth would go through, whether Mark Harmon liked it or not, and the sooner she could get away from this island, the better.

Acutely aware of the atmosphere, she turned and looked helplessly at Laura Harmon.

'I'm sorry. I didn't intend — I didn't want — '

'It's all right,' the older woman broke in soothingly, laying a reassuring hand on her arm. She had recovered her composure and was her brisk self again. Tansy felt a surge of relief at the knowledge that Mark Harmon's mother, despite her loyalty to him, had not turned against her. She had liked her instinctively from the start, feeling her overtures of friendship were sincere. She had hoped that in Laura Harmon she had at least one friend on the island. Her only one, perhaps . . .

'Please don't feel you have to leave,' the older woman protested now, as Tansy rose to her feet.

'It would be best, I think,' Tansy told her. 'Perhaps we could talk more about things in the morning, when we're all feeling a little calmer.' She hurried towards the door, wanting only to get away from the atmosphere. She had enjoyed the evening, to her surprise, and would have given anything to have avoided the way it had ended. But the sooner she was away from Mark Harmon, the better. She couldn't trust herself not to say more things she would regret later. He had said nothing for the last few moments, his back firmly turned to her, as she saw when she cast a glance at him before stepping into the hallway.

'I did enjoy the evening and the meal was wonderful. Thank you.' She spoke sincerely, when Laura Harmon brought her wrap a few moments later.

'It was our pleasure.' Opening the door, Laura eyed her tentatively. 'Perhaps you'll call down in the morning for coffee? It would be so nice to have a chat, just the two of us.'

'I'd like that,' Tansy said warmly. As she turned to leave, the older woman touched her arm, detaining her, and she turned, eyeing her enquiringly.

'When I said I thought you were like your grandfather, I meant it,' Laura said after a moment's hesitation. 'Not just in looks. In every way. You're a Whitton, all right.'

Tansy frowned. She had no doubt the words were sincerely meant, yet the last thing she wanted to hear was that she and Benson Whitton were alike.

'If you don't mind my mentioning it, you've seemed bemused by the fact that he left his business to you.' Laura spoke hesitantly.

Tansy glanced at her in surprise, marvelling at her intuition.

'I was,' she said frankly. 'And I still haven't come up with a good reason for that. I know I'm his granddaughter but — '

'Perhaps I could venture one.' Laura spoke cautiously. 'And it's what I've just said; that you are so like him.'

'How could he have known that? We never met,' Tansy said.

'He knew all about you, though, and followed your progress in advertising,' Laura responded.

'You mean he kept tabs on me?' Tansy's eyes glinted. 'That doesn't surprise me, knowing what I do of him.'

'Some day you might come to see — ' Laura broke off, biting her lip.

'Yes? What might I come to see?' Tansy eyed her challengingly. 'What a dear, sweet old man he was?'

'Sweet isn't a word I'd have used to describe him.' A brief smile touched the older woman's face. 'But one day you may come to realize that things weren't exactly the way you saw them; that there might, perhaps, have been extenuating circumstances — '

'There can be no extenuating circumstances for wrecking my parents' marriage and causing my father's heart attack,' Tansy responded bluntly. 'But I do appreciate your loyalty to him, Laura. Just as I hope you appreciate mine to my mother. And my father. Goodnight, Laura.'

'Miss Forrester!'

About to step outside, Tansy turned at the sound of Mark Harmon's voice. Unnoticed by either woman, he had made his way into the hallway. Now he stood just inside the door frame, his eyes meeting Tansy's. There was no friendliness in his glance.

'Yes?' Tansy spoke coolly. There was no way she was going to be intimidated by this man.

'I hope I made myself clear enough.' Ignoring his mother's disapproving eyes, he spoke bitingly. 'I am not going to allow you to throw away the livelihood of all the employees at the nursery. You are not going to sell us out to the likes of Paul Tregarth.'

'Oh?' Tansy eyed him defiantly. 'And how do you propose to stop me, Mr Harmon?'

'I don't know,' he admitted grimly. 'But I will stop you, somehow or other. You are not going to turn your grandfather's legacy into a golf-course for Tregarth — '

'Why don't we wait and see what Tregarth has in mind for the nurseries?' Tansy spoke reasoningly.

'I know exactly what he has in mind!' Mark Harmon grated. 'And it is not going to happen.' The vehemence in his voice unnerved Tansy momentarily. What could he do to stop her? Technically, nothing. Yet here on this island, surrounded by people who in all probability saw her as an interloper and a threat to their way of life, she realized suddenly how vulnerable her position was. Mark Harmon's words, and the coldness in his eyes, left her in no doubt whatsoever that he would do everything in his power to thwart her in her intention of selling Whitton Lodge Nurseries to Paul Tregarth.

2

Tansy spent a restless night in the unfamiliar bed. Used to the roar of the city's traffic, she found the silence of her surroundings unnerving and was up early the following morning, breakfasted and ready for whatever the day might bring. The click of the letter-box had her hurrying into the hallway, though as expected, the mail consisted mainly of circulars and business post concerning the nurseries. A smile curved her mouth, however, as she recognized her mother's handwriting on one of the envelopes. Putting the rest of the mail down on the hallway table, she headed back towards the living-room, tearing her mother's letter open eagerly as she did so.

'I got your letter this morning,' she read. 'And I felt I had to write back straight away. I wish you hadn't decided to go to Calanara, Tansy. But since you have, I feel that before you pick up a garbled version of what happened all those years ago, I must do what I should have done a long time ago, and tell you the truth . . . '

Tansy's fingers shook as she read her mother's letter. At last, she was about to learn the answers to questions which had puzzled her more and more since coming to the island. The doorbell shrilled suddenly, startling her. When it sounded again, more insistently, she pushed the letter into her pocket with a sigh of annoyance and hurried back into the hallway. She had to make an effort at politeness, recalling their argument of the previous evening, when she opened the door to find Mark Harmon standing there. His greeting, too, was only just within the boundaries of courtesy.

'I thought you might like to see round the nurseries this morning,' he said coolly. 'It would be a pity not to see them before handing them over to Tregarth.'

Tansy's mouth tightened. By the look of it, he was determined to maintain the hostility which had flared so suddenly between them. Well, at least she knew where she stood with him.

'I'd love to see the nurseries.' Her tone matched his. 'There are some circulars and things here, by the way.' Picking up the remainder of the post, she handed it to him. 'Won't you come in?' she added with studied politeness.

'I'd rather we got on our way, if you don't mind.' He moved restlessly. 'I'm expecting an important telephone call down at the office. You've had breakfast, I hope?'

Tansy hesitated, her mind still on her mother's letter. She badly wanted to finish reading it, but not with him looking on with those disapproving eyes of his. Whatever the truth was concerning her grandfather's and her mother's estrangement, it was something she wanted to read in private. It looked, though, as if it would have to wait a while.

He was tapping the door now in a barely concealed gesture of impatience and there was nothing for it but to collect her things from the hallway cloak cupboard and follow him. There was silence between them on the short drive between the Lodge and the nurseries. Overhead, the sun slanted through the window, bathing the scene in its glow. Ahead of them sprawled the nursery buildings, beyond which the hills were clearly visible now that the early morning mist had lifted. Tansy eyed the scene before her hesitantly now, uncertain of the reception awaiting her from the nursery employees. Any sense of obligation she might have felt towards them was satisfied by the efforts she was making to see that their jobs were secure. Yet coming face to face with them was not something to which she looked forward, particularly in view of the tales Mark Harmon would undoubtedly have told them about her. She had no illusions about how they would view her, the stranger from the city, interested only in how much money she could make from the sales of the property and not particularly worried about where that money came from.

The thought sparked irritation within her. Why couldn't these people try to see things from her point of view? She had a career and was succeeding in a highly competitive area, yet because Benson Whitton had beckoned from beyond the grave, she was expected to forget all that and bury herself here on this tiny, if enchanting, island. If only things were that simple! How could she make them understand how she felt about owning anything of her grandfather's, without arousing their anger? It was obvious that Benson Whitton had been a revered figure around here. They had seen another side of him, by all accounts; a side which he had not shown to his son-in-law, nor his daughter, once she had gone against his wishes. She saw the old man in a different way from them, and they would somehow have to accept that. The visit would be embarrassing for her, she acknowledged now, yet it was something which she could handle. She just wished she could have had more time to prepare for it. She became aware of Mark Harmon's swift glance in her direction, as he brought the vehicle to a halt outside the main greenhouse.

'Ready?' he murmured.

It was an innocent enough query, yet Tansy was aware of the undercurrent behind it.

'I'm ready,' she responded. *For anything with which you choose to confront me . . .*

People could be seen, absorbed in their work, as they entered the greenhouse. Tansy looked around her with interest, as they made their way down the long aisle. Plants and trays of cuttings were piled on the counters on either side of her and the whole effect was of a blaze of colour.

'This is Joe Traynor, our head

nurseryman.' Mark had stopped now near an elderly, whitecoated man, who left his work immediately and approached them, hand outstretched towards Tansy, his face creased in a smile.

'Welcome to you, Miss Forrester,' he said.

'Hello, Joe.' Tansy's voice held an answering warmth as she gripped his hand.

Stepping back towards the counter, he picked up a white carnation and handed it to her.

'I prepared this in the hope that you would come,' he told her. 'I did a button-hole for your grandfather every morning, and I hope you will allow me to continue the custom,' he added.

'Thank you.' Moved by the old man's unexpected courtly gesture, Tansy's voice was gentle. 'It's beautiful.'

'We'll leave you to it, Joe.' With a nod, Mark Harmon drew Tansy further down the aisle. Her expression was thoughtful. She had been prepared for wariness from the staff — hostility, even

— and the genuine warmth of the old man's welcome had taken her by surprise.

'He always did have a way with the ladies,' Mark said drily, once they were out of earshot.

'Has he been with the nurseries long?' Tansy asked.

'He came here as an apprentice,' he answered.

'That long?' Tansy spoke involuntarily.

'Oh yes.' He eyed her shrewdly. 'Did you think that the workforce would be entirely comprised of highly trained graduates from the top horticultural colleges? We have one of two students here, naturally, spending some time as part of their course, but in the main, our employees were taken on years ago and trained up. Those who showed exceptional ability were sent on courses at the nursery's expense, either locally or in the city. Heather is a case in point. She was a relative, of course, but apart from that, she's very talented. She seems to have inherited the Whitton green fingers.'

'Unlike me?' Tansy couldn't help murmuring.

'I wasn't making any particular point,' he responded. 'You did express an interest in the employees; sorry if I elaborated too much for you.'

Tansy stifled her annoyance at his inference that her interest in the business was only mercenary. And she couldn't help wondering again if he resented the fact that her grandfather had left the nurseries to her instead of to Heather. What had the old man hoped to gain by leaving the business to her, she wondered? Surely his intention could not have been to drive a wedge between herself and her mother, perhaps in retaliation for her mother's past actions? Was he that ruthless? Or had it been a whim on his part, a fleeting gesture of reconciliation? Tansy sighed. The image she had long held of a stern, unbending tyrant who brought the full force of his wrath down on anyone who opposed him, was more and more at variance with the picture the people here presented of a man concerned for the welfare of his employees, and who rewarded loyalty with his own. Which was the real Benson Whitton? Had he mellowed with age, learned the hard lesson that if he treated people badly, they would leave him? Or had her mother's judgement, already clouded by loyalty to her husband, become warped over the years to the extent of turning him into a monster in the eyes of his granddaughter? Again, she wished she'd had time to read the letter from her mother before Mark Harmon had arrived on the scene.

'This is Tom Barnes, our apprentice, and Carl Wharton, who's one of the students I mentioned earlier.'

She came back to the present to find that Mark Harmon was introducing her to two young men at the far end of the greenhouse. They acknowledged her greeting shyly. At last, Tansy and Mark left the cool greenhouse and moved back into the warmth of the early morning sun. Tansy couldn't resist a sigh of relief. So far, so good. There couldn't be many more people to meet . . .

'Mark!'

At the sound of the voice they both turned to see Heather Parker emerging from a small hut which evidently served as an office.

'The telephone call I was waiting for. It must be coming through,' Mark exclaimed.

'Yes; they're on the line now,' Heather confirmed. As she drew nearer to them, she nodded briefly to Tansy then turned her attention back to Mark. 'I told them to hold on,' she informed him.

'Good.' He looked enquiringly at Tansy. 'If you'll excuse me a moment — '

'Go ahead,' Tansy interrupted quickly. 'Don't let me interfere with things.'

He hurried towards the hut and moments later she heard his crisp tones speaking into the telephone. Left alone with Heather, she was aware suddenly of the constraint in the atmosphere. The other girl was avoiding her eyes, obviously ill at ease, yet reluctant to show rudeness by walking away from her. It only served to confirm what Tansy had already sensed the previous evening, that Heather was not happy with her presence on the island. She had some sympathy for her, guessing the other girl saw her as a threat to her relationship with Mark Harmon; added, perhaps, to resentment at Tansy's acquisition of the nurseries. The silence lengthened, threatening to become an embarrassment, and she searched for some remark with which to break it.

'Everything seems to be going well here.' She made a determined effort at brightness.

'Yes.' Heather's response was a little forced. 'Mark's a good manager. My uncle trusted him completely.'

Tansy couldn't help wondering if the other girl's reference to Benson Whitton as her uncle had been made innocently, or if it had been a deliberate attempt to make her feel even more of an outsider than she already did. Winning Heather Parker over would not be easy, bearing in mind the other girl's double reason for resenting her. She eyed Heather speculatively now, wondering how she would react to questions about her uncle.

'So your father — or is it mother? — was my grandfather's second cousin?' she ventured.

'That's right,' Heather responded. 'We live over the other side of the island.'

'Perhaps I'll have a chance to meet them before I leave,' Tansy murmured. She looked across in relief as Mark Harmon came out of the office. There was a smile on his face and it included both of them.

'Looks as if we've clinched a deal with a supermarket on the mainland to provide all their horticultural requirements,' he said.

'Mark! So you did it!' Heather

exclaimed, her pleasure evident.

'It's only verbal yet, but we'll be receiving confirmation and a contract shortly,' he said.

'It's wonderful news,' Tansy said warmly. 'Congratulations!'

'Thanks.' In the light of the good news, his manner towards her had thawed somewhat, yet there was an unspoken message in his eyes. *The jubilation might be short-lived, if Tregarth takes over the nurseries . . . .* He glanced at Heather.

'I'd like to carry on and show Miss Forrester the rest of the property, if you can hold the fort here.'

'Of course.' Heather's reply was made quickly, yet Tansy thought she detected an edge to her voice.

'If things are busy — ' she was beginning, when Mark Harmon interrupted firmly.

'Heather's perfectly capable of running things. We can't have you going back to the city without seeing the full extent of your domain. Besides, there's something special I wanted you to see.' As he spoke, he was leading the way down the gravel path, apparently heading towards open countryside. A slight breeze rose as they moved away from the shelter of the buildings and Tansy drew her anorak round her, her bewilderment increasing as they continued. What was this something special he was going to such pains to show her, she wondered? The hills had taken on a bluish hue, and though they could not see the sea from that distance, Tansy's nostrils caught the tang of it in the air. To one side, meadows stretched like a patchwork quilt, whilst to the other, distant buildings and a church spire were evidence of the island's main town. Hurrying to keep up with his long strides, Tansy eyed him enquiringly.

'Where are we going?'

For answer, he turned to the right and headed towards a gate. Following, Tansy saw that it led into a small meadow.

'Here it is,' he said softly. 'The real reason Paul Tregarth wants to get his hands on Whitton Lodge Nurseries.' Pride jostled with satisfaction in his voice.

Tansy stared at the scene before her. At first glance, it looked like any other meadow to her city-bred eyes. Then, gradually, she became aware of a waving mass of colour as far as her eye could see. The sun's rays glinted on plants of every description and colour, prominent among them the white and silver petals of Merlin's Tears. The whole effect was that of a moving mosaic.

'A wild flower meadow,' Mark spoke quietly then, aware of her questioning gaze. 'Your grandfather had this meadow seeded with every wild flower he could get hold of. It's one of the few places left where you can see so many species growing together.'

Tansy was silent for several moments. 'It's beautiful,' she said at last.

'Isn't it?' he murmured. 'Your grandfather was conservation minded, as many of us are, on Calanara.' He glanced down at her. 'Would you like to hear how much Tregarth offered him for this meadow?'

Tansy was silent.

'A great deal of money,' he said softly, when it became obvious she wasn't going to respond. 'And not out of sympathy with conservationists, I assure you. As you can see, the meadow is adjacent to Tregarth's property. Owning it is vital to him, if he wants to expand his existing golf-course. But your grandfather turned down his offer without hesitation.'

Tansy's thoughts were in confusion, in the light of these revelations. The feelings which had been forcing themselves into her mind about her grandfather since arriving on the island were becoming stronger, resolving themselves into questions which demanded answers. Was a man who valued wild flowers above large sums of money capable of wrecking his daughter's life? Had his nature been so complex that the survival of these flowers meant more to him than the survival of his only child's marriage?

Mark Harmon was watching her now, aware of her conflicting emotions and evidently expecting some sort of response. And there was only one response she could make. She would have had to be totally devoid of any normal feelings not to say what she felt he wanted to hear. And she realized then why he had brought her here.

'I won't let Paul Tregarth destroy this meadow,' she assured him. 'I promise you that.'

He gave a cynical laugh and she looked at him, startled.

'Don't you believe me?' she asked.

'Oh yes, I believe you,' he responded, sobering. 'But if you think Tregarth would leave this meadow intact, once you've sold out to him, you're naive.'

Tansy sought in her mind for a solution. 'I'll have a clause written into the agreement,' she insisted.

'It wouldn't work!' he said impatiently. 'Not with Tregarth! He's not the normal, honest-to-goodness businessman, take it from me.'

'Aren't you prejudging him a little?' Tansy demanded. 'What dealings have you had with him to back up your opinion of him? Isn't it just that you don't want the nurseries to go into another owner's hands; that you won't be able to run things the way you're used to doing — '

'There'll be nothing left *to* run, if Tregarth gets his hands on the place,' he interrupted savagely. 'Can't you get that through your head? Anyway — ' He moved restlessly. ' — contrary to what you might be thinking, I didn't bring you down here to have another argument with you. I just wanted you to see your heritage — and what you'd be destroying when you hand it over to Tregarth.'

Turning, he walked back in the direction of the greenhouse, and after a moment, Tansy followed him. It hadn't been fair of him, she thought, taking her down to see that meadow. Yet could she blame him for using every means in his power to persuade her not to sell out? The silence between them gave her an opportunity to ponder on the implications of the visit to the meadow. Obviously, she could not allow Paul Tregarth to destroy it. Despite Mark Harmon's scepticism, she felt sure she could come to some agreement with Tregarth; she had to! But that wasn't her only concern now. Everything she had heard about her grandfather since coming to the island, culminating in his desire to preserve the wild flower meadow, contradicted her long held beliefs about him. The facts didn't fit.

They were nearing the Land Rover now, and Tansy couldn't help but feel relief that the tour was over. Mark Harmon's expression was troubled as he climbed in and waited for her to settle herself in the passenger seat. There was a constraint between them now, Tansy felt, which was almost as bad as the open antagonism he had shown earlier. At least she could deal with that. Had the meadow been his final trump card, she wondered? And if so, knowing now that it had not had the desired effect of making her abandon her intention to sell out, was he about to accept defeat and make the best of the situation? Eyeing his grim expression, she doubted it. As they headed out of the nursery grounds and turned in the opposite direction to Whitton Lodge, Tansy eyed him in surprise.

'Aren't we going back?'

He shook his head. 'I thought, since I've made myself your guide, I'd show you some of the island,' he told her. 'It's a lovely day for a drive, don't you think?' He eyed her enquiringly, and she shrugged.

'I don't want to monopolize your time,' she said at last. 'You said it was a hectic period for the nurseries.'

'I'm entitled to a break,' he told her. 'And what could be more important than taking care of the boss?'

Despite the bantering remark, his voice was without its customary sarcasm; almost, she felt, as if he had stated his case for not selling the nurseries, and was now prepared to let it stand on its merits. She was only too willing to let things be. Being on bad terms with her late grandfather's employees was not something she welcomed. Watching through the window, she noticed that they were heading back to the coast, the hills in the distance becoming more discernible. The ground was rising, flat meadows giving way to woodland. Sunlight slanted through tall trees and above the noise of the Land Rover's engine she caught the sound of birdsong. She looked around her, entranced, as the island fell away and the road climbed through wooded slopes. Far below, the sea twinkled, reflecting the sun like a silver cloak. Wild flowers dotted the slope, predominant among them the distinctive flowers of Merlin's Tears. She caught her breath then, realizing where he was taking her. Noting her expression, he nodded.

'So you guessed,' he said. 'Look!' Leaning his head towards the window on Tansy's side, he pointed upwards. 'See that opening up there in the hillside?'

Following his pointing finger, Tansy squinted upwards. For a few moments she looked around her, then her eyes alighted on the place he was indicating. It appeared to be the mouth of a cavern some yards from where the hillside dropped away towards the distant shore. Turning, her eyes questioned him, and he nodded.

'Merlin's Cavern,' he confirmed.

Turning back, Tansy looked upwards eagerly, recalling the story she had heard the previous evening. She had not imagined she would be able to visit the spot in the short time she would be on the island; now, she had a feeling of anticipation as they drew nearer. There was a peaceful atmosphere here which, she noticed when she left the vehicle moments later, caught her off guard. She couldn't help marvelling, too, at how much the island had affected her in the short time she had been on it. What, for instance, was she doing now, taking seriously a legend she had been told about an old wizard who hadn't even existed, according to some people? In the city, she would have listened with polite interest, then dismissed it from her mind. Here, it could so easily seem real . . . Looking around, she saw that the ground was carpeted now with the white and silver flowers of Merlin's Tears, twinkling jewel-bright in the sun, thickest near the mouth of the cavern.

'So this is it.' Her eyes were thoughtful as she gazed at the entrance to the cavern. 'Wasn't there a stone blocking the entrance in the story?'

'It *is* only a legend, and the details have become somewhat lost in time,' he murmured.

'It's a sad little tale,' Tansy said involuntarily.

'But not without its moral,' he responded. He gave her a swift glance. 'There's no fool like an old fool?' he suggested, when she eyed him question-ingly. 'And not only the old ones,' he added quietly. 'There's many a younger man been made a fool of by a woman.'

Tansy ignored the comment, sensing its inference. From the start, he had cast her in the mould of heartless career woman who cared nothing for the interests of the people who worked at Whitton Lodge Nurseries. That had been his motive for taking her round the place, she felt sure; so that these people whom he imagined she saw as statistics would become real to her. Then, the softening up process begun, he had brought her up here to this lovely place, hoping, perhaps, that its intangible associations with an enchanted legend would move her where mascu-line logic had failed.

'You're very like your grandfather; did you know that?' he asked suddenly, watching her.

Tansy sighed. 'Your mother said the same thing,' she reminded him. 'Per-sonally, I don't see it as the compliment you obviously feel it is.'

'Why do you hate him so much?' he asked abruptly.

'Hate him?' she echoed. 'How could I hate him? I never met him — as you are so quick to point out at every opportunity.'

'Didn't it ever occur to you that there might have been two sides to the argument?' he persisted.

'I was never interested in hearing his side of it,' Tansy acknowledged honestly. 'Perhaps that was wrong of me, but my loyalties were to my parents. Do you know the details?' She eyed him enquiringly.

'Only the bare bones,' he admitted. 'Your mother married against his wishes.'

'It's rather more than that,' Tansy told him. 'He refused to help my father out of a financial mess, though he obviously had the means to do so.'

'He believed in people standing on their own feet,' he pointed out.

'Sometimes it isn't possible to get out

of something on one's own.' Tansy spoke stiffly. The remark had sounded like criticism of her father. 'Anyway, he had a heart attack as a result of the whole thing and died.'

Mark Harmon eyed her thoughtfully. 'I'm sorry about that,' he said at last. 'But Benson couldn't have foreseen that would happen. And despite what you say, I know there has to be more to it. He was a hard man, but he'd never have stood by and watched your father struggle, without a good reason. I knew him well enough to be able to say that.'

Tansy was aware of a strong urge to take her mother's letter from her pocket and read it. It was there; the truth behind all this. Yet she resisted the impulse. The man beside her was too partisan, too much on her grandfather's side for her to trust him yet with the information the letter contained. Yet wasn't she attributing to him things which she herself was guilty of, too? If he was too much her grandfather's supporter, hadn't she, in her turn, appointed herself her parents' advocate a long time ago and refused to even consider that there might be more to the affair than she was prepared to look for?

'I might be wrong but — ' he hesitated. 'Well, I feel since coming here, you've begun to probe; to want to get at the truth of what happened, instead of continuing to accept the version of events you've grown up with. That's what he would have wanted, I think. In fact, of all the reasons I've told myself he left the business to you, I'm beginning to think that's the main one.' His voice took on a reflective note. 'In fact, the more I think about it, the surer I am that Benson knew that, once you came to the island, you'd want to find out for yourself what the truth was. Maybe that's all he wanted; to be vindicated in your eyes.'

'How could he be so sure I'd even come to the island?' Tansy challenged.

'I don't know,' he admitted frankly. 'But you did come, didn't you?'

'Only to sell up,' Tansy reminded him. 'I haven't changed my mind about that.' Yet, her voice was troubled. Seeing the wild flower meadow had shaken her resolve a little, though she still felt sure she could get Paul Tregarth to agree to its preservation. She eyed Mark Harmon speculatively. The urge to read her mother's letter was becoming overwhelming, and she was aware of a feeling of dishonesty in continuing the conversation, when the answers to both their questions were so near. Despite their antagonism towards each other, she had judged Mark Harmon to be honest in his dealings, his loyalty steadfast towards those to whom he chose to give it. That they were on opposing sides in the matter made no difference to that feeling. He had worked in Benson Whitton's interests and she was part of that family, no matter what had happened in the past. She owed it to herself, and to Mark Harmon, to be honest in her turn.

'This morning, when you called at the lodge, I'd just been about to read a

68

letter from my mother which arrived in the morning's post,' she said at last. 'I'd written, telling her I was coming to Calanara, and she had written back immediately. She said I ought to know the truth of what happened. I'd planned to finish reading the letter later, but . . . '

She took the envelope from her pocket now and opened it. Mark Harmon was eyeing her intently.

'If you'd rather I left you to read it . . . ' he murmured.

'No.' Tansy's response was firm. 'The affair concerns us both, after all.' She spread the letter out. 'I'll read it aloud. She begins by wishing I hadn't decided to come here, then goes on — ' She cleared her throat. ''I'll start at the beginning, Tansy, and when I've finished, you must judge for yourself the actions of everyone concerned. As you know, your father was an artist, spending the summer on Calanara, helping out at the nurseries in his spare time to earn his keep. I had been away until late in the summer and when I returned, I met your father. We fell in love, Tansy. I knew he'd been seeing another girl — an employee at the nurseries — before I came back to the island. But it was all finished when he and I started going together. We had a brief courtship, Tansy. I soon knew your father was the man I wanted to spend my life with, and he felt the same about me. My father was very much opposed to our marrying, feeling we should wait a while. But I was twenty-one and I didn't need his permission to marry. When he heard about our marriage plans, he did all he could to prevent us going ahead. At first I didn't understand why; it was only later that I learned that the girl your father had been going with before he met me was pregnant by him.'' Tansy's voice trailed off momentarily. She was aware of a feeling of shock, and it was all she could do to carry on.

''Your father told me he hadn't known about the pregnancy. I believed

70

him and still do, to this day. But my father wouldn't believe it. He had a strong sense of duty towards his employees and was outraged that I intended going ahead with my wedding plans. He felt your father should marry the other girl and acknowledge the child as his own. I couldn't lose him, Tansy. I loved him and would have supported him in anything. I wanted him on any terms and he wanted me. Rightly or wrongly, nothing else mattered to either of us. We carried on with our plans to marry. My father — your grandfather — took charge of everything; arranged for the girl to go away whilst she had her baby, and so on. You must remember that things were different in those days; it was a terrible thing for a girl, having an illegitimate child, particularly on a small island like this. So much so, she ran off after the child's birth; abandoned it. We heard later that she had married and was living abroad. Your grandfather arranged for the baby to be fostered, I understand, by some people on the island. You may be wondering why your father and I didn't take the child then and bring it up as our own. But it was settled with its foster-parents, had been adopted in fact, and we'd had you. It wouldn't have been fair. And to be honest, I didn't want that other woman's child around, a constant reminder of your father's involvement with her. I knew my father would do everything he could for the child, and it seemed better to let things go on as they were.'' Tansy glanced away, hardly able to take it all in. Returning to the letter, she scanned the last few pages. ''So now you know the truth and you must judge us all as you see fit. My father judged me; he stood by and never raised a finger to help when your father got into financial difficulties with the art gallery. Of course, he wasn't to know that the stress of it all would bring on your father's fatal heart attack, but I could never forgive him and I hold him indirectly responsible for your father's death and will do, to my dying day. That's why I never allowed you to meet him. He ruined my life and I was afraid that, given a chance, he might ruin yours. He tried to force me to bring you to the island when you were very young, and now, in death, he's managed to do what I would never allow in his lifetime. He's got you to Calanara. And once there, Tansy, I'm afraid its spell will never let you leave.''

Putting the letter down. Tansy looked into Mark Harmon's eyes, her own huge with shock and horror.

'How awful,' she said at last. It was something she had never expected to read. A child, abandoned by its own mother and father; *her* father. A child, in all probability still living somewhere on this island, who was her half-brother or -sister . . .

3

'How could they do it?' Tansy's voice shook. 'That baby — rejected like that by everyone — '

'Not quite everyone,' Mark Harmon interrupted. He had listened without comment as she read the letter aloud. Now he eyed her compellingly. 'Your grandfather didn't turn his back on the child.'

'That's right.' Wonder mingled with Tansy's other emotions. 'He was the only one who faced up to the situation. If it hadn't been for him, that poor child . . . ' Her voice trailed off.

So at last, out of the blue, after all her attempts to get at the truth, here it was. It was a sad, harrowing tale, and no one emerged from it with any credit. Her view of her parents was muddled; torn between love for them and anger for what they had done, she could only wrestle impotently with her confused emotions. There *had* been more to it, as Mark Harmon had hinted. She could imagine it all so well; the girl, pregnant and abandoned by her lover; her own mother clinging desperately to the man she loved beyond all else, not caring what happened so long as he stayed with her. Her father, turning his back on his responsibilities, leaving it all in her grandfather's hands. And her grandfather himself; knowing now the loyalty and concern he felt for his employees, she could imagine his feelings at what he saw as the betrayal of one of them by his own prospective son-in-law. The anger he must have felt, coupled with the knowledge that his daughter would not, like himself, wash her hands of him, would have been a hard thing to bear. And when a few years later, her father had found himself in financial difficulties, Benson Whitton would have viewed it as just retribution, and in his bitterness, done nothing to help.

Even now, she could hardly believe that somewhere on Calanara there was someone who, though a complete stranger, was so closely related to her. How she wished her mother had been more specific! Had the child been a boy or a girl? She felt sure her mother had told her all she knew, once she had decided to unburden herself, yet she was frustrated by the limited amount of knowledge the letter had contained. She couldn't help feeling appalled at the lack of interest her mother had shown in the child her husband had fathered before marrying her. It was possible that only by ignoring the facts had she been able to live with the knowledge of it. And what about him? How could he have turned his back on his own child like that? What kind of a man had he been? She remembered him as a loving father, yet even then he had known of his other child's existence and apparently chosen to ignore the fact. Despite that, she still thought of him with love and made an effort now not to judge him. Who knew what kind of pressure had been brought to bear on him by her mother, because she was afraid of losing him? Viewed now from the distance of time, the events seemed hardly real, but there was no doubt that her mother's letter had told the truth. No wonder she had been at pains to conceal the facts for as long as possible! Only the fear of Tansy's hearing a possibly distorted version of events from another source had prompted her to speak out now! And how was it possible to distort the facts, Tansy wondered? They were brutal enough, as it was. The more Tansy thought about the unknown child, the more her curiosity burned.

'I must find the child, Mark.' She eyed him tentatively. 'Perhaps your mother would know something about it?'

'Perhaps,' he agreed. 'If anyone would have heard anything, it would be her. But don't count on her telling you, even if she does know anything. Like the rest of us, she sets great store by loyalty. And presumably Benson didn't want the child traced, for its own sake.'

'Surely we both have a right to know of each other's existence?' Tansy asked.

'As far as I'm concerned, you have,' he responded. 'But others may see things differently.'

'Why? I'm not out to do the child any harm,' Tansy protested. 'For heaven's sake, it's my brother or sister we're talking about!'

'Half-brother or -sister,' he corrected. 'And it's just possible whoever he or she is might not want to know whose child he really was — always supposing he or she doesn't already know.'

'Surely they'd have come forward if they had known?' Tansy asked.

'And the fact that they didn't might have its own interpretation,' Mark pointed out.

'In other words, he or she doesn't want to be found,' Tansy challenged. 'Is that what you're saying?'

'That's exactly what I'm saying,' he

confirmed. 'I'm not trying to be a pessimist, but I don't want anyone getting hurt in all this; either you or the child.' He eyed her appraisingly. 'Have you considered that your motives might be a little selfish?' he ventured then. 'That you just want to find your half-brother or -sister?'

'I only know I have to find the child,' Tansy insisted. 'Anyone with any normal feelings would want to do that.' She moved restlessly then, wanting to leave. In the face of the letter's revelations, all thoughts of exploring Merlin's Cavern had disappeared from her mind. All she could think of was getting back to the nurseries and questioning Laura Harmon. Sensing her feelings, Mark turned and within minutes they were heading back down to where he had parked the Land Rover.

The journey back held none of its earlier fascination for Tansy. Her thoughts were preoccupied with the things she had learned from the letter.

She viewed the nursery buildings which came into sight some time later with barely concealed impatience. Increasing speed, Mark turned the Landrover into the lane which led to Gatehouse Cottage.

'I'm sure you're dying to question my mother, and she'll be glad to see you again,' he murmured. 'You two seem to get on well together.'

Laura was pottering about in the front garden when they drew up by the gate. Putting down her tools, she came towards them, smiling.

'Laura — ' Tansy was out of the Land Rover almost before Mark had brought it to a stop. 'I've discovered the truth about my grandfather's and my parents' quarrel!'

'Oh?' Laura eyed her shrewdly. 'Come inside. I'll make some tea.'

Quickly, Tansy filled the other woman in on the details of the letter as they walked into the house together.

'Think of it, Laura!' Tansy's eyes smouldered with excitement. 'I have a half-brother or -sister somewhere on this island.' Catching sight of the older woman's expression, she frowned. Laura didn't look surprised, and suddenly Tansy knew why. 'You knew, didn't you?' she accused.

'I did hear that the girl had become pregnant, but nothing else.' Laura touched Tansy's arm in a conciliatory gesture. 'It was all hushed up very quickly. And telling you would have breached your grandfather's confidence.' Her eyes were compelling. 'Forgive me, Tansy. It was your mother's story to tell in any case, not mine.'

Tansy sighed. That unquenchable loyalty again . . .

'I understand,' she said at last.

Mark had followed them into the house. Now he eyed Tansy warningly. 'Don't rush too quickly ahead with this,' he advised. 'You may find yourself stirring up a hornet's nest.'

'But it's only natural I should want to find out what happened to the baby,'

Tansy pointed out.

'Of course it is,' he agreed. 'All I'm saying is take things slowly. This is a very close-knit community and people might not like you poking around. I'll ask one or two people I know, first. Under no circumstances should you go around questioning complete strangers.'

'I wouldn't dream of doing that!' Tansy protested. 'I could find out easily enough by looking up the records, in any case.'

'You can't do that until you have the mother's name,' Mark pointed out. 'Leave it for the moment. Will you do that?'

He eyed her enquiringly and Tansy looked dubiously back at him. They were hardly friendly enough for her to trust him that far and she couldn't help wondering if he were trying to head her off before she picked up the trail. He had been less than enthusiastic from the start about finding her half-brother or -sister.

'You don't trust me, is that it?' His

eyes glinted in her direction. 'I assure you I'm not up to anything devious! I've opposed your plans for the nurseries, that's true, but I've done it openly; made no bones about where I stand. And I have nothing to gain — or lose — by your finding your half-brother or -sister. If anything, I'm quite curious myself about it. So won't you take at least some part of me on trust?'

It was true, Tansy acknowledged. He had been nothing but honest in his dealings with her.

'All right.' She came to a decision. 'I'll leave you to see what you can pick up.'

'Good.' He smiled briefly and, not for the first time, Tansy realized how attractive he was, when he wasn't wearing that scowl with which he had favoured her so much the previous day. She had no wish to make an enemy of him, nor indeed of anyone else on this island. All she wanted to do was conclude her business here and return to her own life on the mainland.

He was talking to his mother now, telling her the news of the supermarket contract, and Tansy listened silently, feeling again that slight uneasiness as she saw the older woman's obvious pleasure at the news. Again, she resolved to do all she could to persuade Paul Tregarth to leave the nurseries running in their present form, if and when he took them over. There must be some way she could ensure that he kept at least part of the business intact.

'I'll get back to the nuseries now,' Mark remarked, taking a swift sip of the tea his mother had handed him. 'I'll see you later.' Turning, he left the room and moments later, the sound of the Land Rover's engine could be heard as it sped back down the lane. Wandering into the living-room, the two women sat in companionable silence. Tansy pondered the events of the morning. Now that she had agreed to leave the question of the baby's identity to Mark Harmon for the time being, her mind could dwell on other matters.

'I won't let Paul Tregarth destroy the wild flower meadow, Laura. Believe me!' She looked entreatingly in the older woman's direction.

'I do.' Laura patted her arm reassuringly. 'I know you wouldn't do anything to harm us; you're a Whitton.'

Tansy was reminded uncomfortably then of the unspoken expectations she had sensed since coming to the island that she would take over her grandfather's place at the helm of Whitton Lodge Nurseries. She hated to disappoint the older woman, but there was no choice. And even if she had been interested in taking over, she felt sure that Mark Harmon would not thank her for it. Despite the fact that he obviously agreed with the general feeling that she should keep the nurseries in the family, he would not want her taking an active role in running things, she sensed. Becoming an absentee owner and leaving him with a free hand was more what he had in mind.

'Why does Mark feel so bitter about Tregarth?' she asked impulsively. 'It can't be just because Tregarth wants to acquire the nursery land, surely?'

Laura frowned. 'It's Tregarth's methods he hates,' she said after a moment. 'We've had intermittent acts of vandalism over the years; nothing too serious so far —— '

'Vandalism?' Tansy eyed her in concern. 'He's said nothing about that! Surely he doesn't think Tregarth is behind it?'

'He has no proof it was instigated by Tregarth,' Laura said bluntly. 'It could be village children or tourists, I suppose. But Mark has always felt Tregarth was behind it.'

'Tregarth's a businessman; he wouldn't stoop to such methods!' Tansy protested.

'Businessmen can be quite unscrupulous when they want something,' Laura pointed out. 'Not that I'm saying I agree with Mark.'

'How often does it happen?' Tansy asked.

'We've had no trouble for a while now; ever since your grandfather became ill, in fact,' Laura told her. 'Presumably Tregarth would have no need to indulge in such methods, once he knew it was merely a matter of waiting for Benson to die; that's if he *was* behind it,' she continued thoughtfully. 'All he had to do was wait and see if whoever inherited the place was more amenable to his offer to buy us out than Benson was.'

If that were true, Tansy thought, she had made things easier for him than he could have imagined ... Later, she made her way back to the Lodge, pausing in surprise when she caught sight of Joe Traynor tending the garden.

'Hello, Joe.' Closing the gate, she turned and smiled at him.

'Morning again, Miss Forrester.' He touched his cap in an old-fashioned gesture of respect. 'I'd a spare moment and there were some bedding plants left over in the greenhouse which I thought would go beautifully in this spot, now the summer annuals are going over.'

'So it's you I have to thank for keeping the garden looking so lovely.' Tansy eyed the riot of colour approvingly.

'It's a job I was proud to do for your grandfather,' he responded. 'And I'll go on doing it whilst a Whitton owns this place.'

Tansy frowned, wondering if there was implied criticism in the remark, or if it was just an old man's view of things. She could hardly expect any of them to be pleased by the news of the impending take-over, yet how could she make them see that it might not be the disaster they were all convinced it would be?

'You'll all be offered jobs, Joe,' she pointed out. 'If the nurseries change hands.'

He paused in his work, his weather-beaten face creased in uncertainty. 'If you say so, miss,' he murmured.

Hearing him, Tansy sighed. 'I do say so. I have Mr Tregarth's assurances on it,' she said patiently. 'What about some coffee?' she asked then, determinedly changing the subject.

A smile lit up his face. 'That would be extremely kind,' he told her.

'Right; I'll get that moving,' she promised, turning in the direction of the Lodge. It was little enough, she felt, when put side by side with the old man's utter devotion to her late grandfather and everything connected with him.

The sun was coming through when she returned to the garden some time later, carrying a laden tray, and she lingered, reluctant to go back inside the gloomy house. Smiling his thanks, the old man took the coffee she held out to him. Perching herself on the garden wall, she took a sip from her own cup, and a companionable silence grew up between them.

'Mark — Mr Harmon — was telling me you'd been here since you were a boy,' she ventured, eyeing him.

He nodded, his expression becoming reminiscent.

'I've served your grandfather almost all my life,' he told her. 'A finer man or fairer employer I couldn't have wished to find.'

Tansy looked down at her cup. She had no need of the reminder of how much she had misjudged her grandfather.

'I wish I could have met him.' She spoke softly, impulsively. 'It was all so needless — ' she broke off, wondering how much Joe knew of the events of long ago.'

' 'Tweren't your fault.' His tone was gruff. 'It's just something that happened between your mother and Mr Whitton that shouldn't have been allowed to go on, if you don't mind my saying so, miss.'

She eyed him. He knew more about those times than she had realized. Did he, perhaps, know about the baby?

'How much do you know of all that, Joe?' she asked tentatively.

His expression seemed to close up. 'Not much,' he said. 'Mr Whitton didn't confide in me, miss — and I wasn't one for idle gossip.'

He knew more than he was prepared to tell, Tansy felt sure; if not from her grandfather, then from other sources. He would have been working here at the same time as the girl whom her father had abandoned. But he would say nothing further on the subject, she judged. Benson Whitton's employees maintained their unswerving loyalty to him, even after his death. And it wasn't fair of her to ask any of them to breach that loyalty, she knew. There were other, more usual channels she could explore. Yet she had promised Mark Harmon that she would wait to see if he found out anything, and she would honour her promise.

'What do you think about the proposed takeover, Joe?' she asked, changing the subject. 'I realize you're not too happy about it, but if you could only try to look to the future — '

'There won't be any future, miss, if

Tregarth gets his hands on the nurseries,' he said flatly. After his recent reticence about the past, he now seemed more than eager to state his opinions on the future, she couldn't help thinking then.

'Tregarth could be planning to invest capital and time in the place, turning it into a thriving concern,' she pointed out.

'He could, at that!' Joe agreed cautiously. 'And if so, I'll tip my hat to him. But it's my belief he won't.'

'*Is* it your belief?' Tansy asked shrewdly. 'Or has Mr Harmon closed everyone's minds to the idea that Tregarth's taking over the nurseries might be a good thing for everyone? Say what you think, Joe!' she urged. Indecision flitted across his face, and instinctively she realized she had hit the nail on the head. Mark Harmon had been influencing the employees, though whether out of genuine concern for the future or to elicit their support against her, she wasn't sure.

'You're Mr Whitton's granddaughter; you won't do anything against us, I'm sure!' Joe's tone was stubborn. 'But I wish you would reconsider, miss. This place has been in Whitton hands for a long time.'

So it was sentiment which motivated him, she thought, not fear of what Tregarth would do. The thought brought relief.

'Everything changes, Joe,' she said gently. 'I wish I could help you to see that.' She sighed, realizing the futility of her words. Joe was old; he had been here for a lifetime. How could he accept the changes Benson Whitton's death would bring about?

'One day,' she said softly. 'This place may have grown into one of the most important horticultural establishment in the land.'

'Mr Harmon says as how Tregarth will turn it into a bowling-green and suchlike.' Joe's tone was uncertain.

Tansy sighed. Mark Harmon had done his work well . . .

'And my home — ' Anxiety

mingled with fear suddenly in the weather-beaten old face, and she looked at him sharply. 'What will become of that, miss? Our cottage is on Whitton land, down by the stream — there's a few of us with cottages there. Mr Whitton leased them to us at a cheap rent; he knew we couldn't afford to pay much. But if Tregarth takes over, what will happen then?' He turned anguished eyes to her, regarding her with mute appeal. Impulsively, she caught at his arm, eyeing him entreatingly.

'I'd no idea, Joe. No one told me.' Her voice shook slightly. 'Your homes will be safe, Joe. I promise you that. Paul Tregarth, if he takes over the nurseries, will not be allowed to touch the cottages. In fact — ' She took a deep breath as a thought occurred to her. 'I'll have to go into the legal side of things, but if there's any chance he'll accept the deal without the cottages being included, you can be sure I'll push for that.'

'Thanks, miss.' He spoke gratefully. 'I know you'll do your best. And now I must get back to work. There's a lot to do; the weeds spring up at this time of year — ' Replacing his cup on the tray, he turned back to his work. Sensing his need to be left alone to collect himself together, Tansy took the tray and walked back towards the house, casting a swift glance over her shoulder as she did so. Crouched by the border, the old man was painstakingly digging out weeds, and for a moment the sight caught at her heart. It had seemed so simple in the beginning, her plan to sell the nurseries and remain uninvolved with the people on Calanara. Yet as time went by, she was finding out that it was anything but simple. Why, she asked herself, not for the first time, had Benson Whitton saddled her with the responsibility for these people? Had he known that her mother, if she'd inherited, would have sold out, lock, stock and barrel, without a qualm, after the way things had gone between the two of them? Why had he been so sure Tansy wouldn't do the same; she was a stranger here after all, despite being his granddaughter. She knew nothing of these people, or their life-style. Yet more and more, she felt as if some force were tugging her, weaving invisible strands around her to anchor her to this place, and it was a feeling which made her uneasy. She didn't belong here.

Unaccountably, she looked at the telephone, a sudden urge coming over her to ring David Firth; make contact with that other world, the one she had temporarily left behind. It would be reassuring to hear his voice, and she needed to check up on the accounts he was minding for her, anyway. She got through to the office with more ease than she had expected, smiling when she heard the cheery tones of Mary Livingstone, the telephonist.

'Tansy! How are you? When are you coming back?' she asked, when Tansy had identified herself.

'Soon, I hope,' Tansy responded. 'This business is taking longer than I expected.'

'It sounds like the middle of nowhere,' Mary commented.

'It's actually quite a nice place,' Tansy defended. 'And the people — well, most of them — are very friendly.' She listened indulgently as Mary chatted, cutting in when she had an opportunity. 'Is David in the office, by any chance, Mary?'

'I think so. I saw him earlier,' the other woman responded. 'Just hold on a moment.'

Tansy waited patiently as the seconds stretched on. Just as she was beginning to wonder what was happening, Mary came back on the line.

'Sorry, Tansy, he's out of the office just now. I was mistaken . . . '

'Oh.' Tansy frowned. To her ears, Mary's voice sounded subdued. And she had seemed so sure David was there.

'Well, never mind. I'll try again later,' she said.

'Yes, do that — '

Was she imagining relief in Mary's voice, she wondered suddenly? It occurred to her then that David probably was in the office, but with his double workload, was too busy to speak to her just now. She'd heard that note in Mary's voice before, when people in the office had asked her to make some excuse in order to avoid speaking to someone who was on the telephone. Not that she minded. David, after all, was doing enough for her already, and she should have known better than to bother him at the office. Later, she would ring him at home. Laura had invited her for a meal that evening, but she had declined, feeling she would be imposing too much on her, and not being particularly keen to spend an evening in Mark Harmon's company, in any case.

Later, she decided on a stroll, eager to see more of the island for herself. Hearing a car behind her, she turned, moving into the side of the lane, smiling as she recognised Heather Parker behind the wheel. Bringing the car to a halt, the other woman leaned out, raising a hand in acknowledgement, yet Tansy had the distinct feeling that she would have driven straight by, if she could have done so without seeming to be rude.

'It's a lovely evening, isn't it?' She spoke pleasantly, determined to evoke some kind of friendly response from the other woman. 'Just finishing work, are you?'

'That's right,' Heather confirmed. 'And you're out seeing something of our island, are you?' The reference to 'our' island gave Tansy the uncomfortable feeling that the other woman had used it deliberately, to emphasize Tansy's position as an outsider.

'Yes. After all, I won't be here long,' she said quickly, hoping that the other woman would pick up the message she was trying to convey. *You've nothing to worry about. I'm as keen to leave as you are to see me go.*

Evidently she did, for her voice held slightly more warmth when she spoke again.

'It's a lovely place, Miss Forrester. I must show you some of its points of interest.'

'That would be nice,' Tansy told her sincerely. 'Perhaps we could get together over a drink or something?'

'If there's time,' Heather murmured. 'I'll speak to Mark about it when I see him tonight. We ought to be able to arrange something.'

Waving, she drove off, leaving Tansy frowning after her. Had it been deliberate, that mention of seeing Mark Harmon tonight; an effort, perhaps, to appraise Tansy of the situation? For some reason she felt annoyance. Heather Parker struck her suddenly as insecure, particularly in the matter of her relationship with Mark Harmon, and the more she saw of her, the stronger that impression became. Surely his attitude towards Tansy, both at dinner the previous evening and earlier today, should have left Heather in no doubt that she had nothing to worry about in that direction? It must have been very evident to her that the possibility of Tansy and Mark Harmon becoming friends, let alone anything closer, was remote. Feeling unaccountably depressed, she turned and made her way back to the Lodge. The prospect of a long, solitary evening ahead was not a welcome one. She wished now she had accepted Laura's invitation, particularly now she knew her son would not be there. The general manager of Whitton Lodge Nurseries was not about to change his social habits for her convenience, by the sound of it. She had dined at his home the previous day; that, so far as he was apparently concerned, fulfilled his obligation towards her.

Letting herself into the Lodge, she walked across to the window. The nursery lights were off now, everything closed up for the night, and she had an inescapable feeling of loneliness. Her thoughts went instinctively to her life on the mainland, and she was reminded of her intention to call David at home. Dialling the number, she waited, half expecting him to be out. Then the receiver was being picked up and she heard his crisp tones.

'David? It's Tansy — '

She got no further, for the line suddenly clicked and was dead. What had happened? Disengaging the line, she listened. There was nothing wrong at this end; the tone was fine. Re-dialling David's number, she waited, frowned as the connection was made. Immediately there was the sound of the engaged tone, and she realized with dismay that he was probably still holding the receiver, as bewildered as she was. Abandoning the attempt to call him for the moment, she went into the kitchen and made herself some coffee. Trying David's number again ten minutes later, she heard the engaged tone once more. His line was busy, and when she tried again half an hour later, it was still busy.

A faint feeling of unease was gnawing

at her by this time. She recalled the impression she'd had when speaking to her office earlier that day of David's being there, despite Mary Livingstone's denials. He had certainly been there this time; she had heard him, spoken to him briefly, managing to identify herself before they were cut off. She caught her breath then. *Had* they been cut off, in fact? And why hadn't he rung her back, once he'd known she was on the line and trying to contact him? He had the Lodge number; she had left it with him in case of any problems with her accounts. She couldn't help feeling then that something was wrong; that David, for some reason, had put down the telephone, once he'd known who the caller was. Was he avoiding speaking to her — and if so, why? Was it her imagination or was something going on back there on the mainland; something she had no knowledge of and no chance of finding out about, stuck here on this island . . .

4

The insistent sound of the telephone ringing penetrated into Tansy's consciousness. Immediately she was sitting up in bed. Could it be David? Silvers of sunlight were poking through the sides of the curtains, and a glance at the bedside clock showed that it was eight-thirty in the morning. Seconds later, she was running lightly downstairs towards the hallway, picking up the receiver and speaking breathlessly into it.

'Hello? Tansy Forrester here.'

'Miss Forrester! Tregarth speaking.'

'Oh, Mr Tregarth.' Initial disappointment at the fact that it wasn't David was banished at the knowledge that Paul Tregarth, her reason for being on Calanara, was in contact at last.

'I'm sorry; I've called too early, by the sound of it.' Her sleepiness must have been evident to him.

'No, it's all right,' Tansy assured him. 'Please carry on.'

'Good.' His tone changed to brisk-ness. 'I arrived back on the island late last night and I'm keen to get things moving with the nurseries as quickly as possible. I take it that suits you?'

'Definitely.' Tansy forced the last vestiges of sleep from her mind. 'I'd like to get back to the city as soon as I can, actually.'

'I can imagine,' he responded. 'Why don't we meet for lunch today and have a preliminary discussion? You're free, I hope?'

'Oh, yes.' She cast her mind back, trying to recall if Mark Harmon had made any plans, relieved when she realized he hadn't. He wouldn't have taken kindly to having them cancelled in favour of a meeting with Paul Tregarth.

'Fine. Around twelve-thirty at the Smugglers' Retreat?' he suggested. 'It's in the main street in town; anyone will direct you, if you're not familiar with it yet.'

'I'll find it,' Tansy told him.

'Fine. I'll see you then.'

He rang off and she made her way thoughtfully back upstairs. Would it be better to say nothing to the Harmons about the meeting, she wondered? It seemed underhand not to tell them and they would have to know sooner or later. She was still undecided when, showered and dressed, she left the Lodge some time later and headed in the direction of the nurseries. She was unsure of her reception. The last thing she wanted to do was give the impression that she was checking up on them, and it was with some hesitancy that she approached the main greenhouse. Glancing through the window, she saw Mark Harmon inside, talking to someone. About to move away, he turned and caught sight of her as she entered the greenhouse. There was a noticeable lack of warmth in his manner when he walked across and spoke to her a few moments later.

'Hello.'

'Good morning.' Aware of the constraint between them, Tansy made an effort to dispel it. 'I'm not getting in the way?'

'Wouldn't matter if you were,' he returned coolly. 'You are the boss, after all.'

Tansy had to make an effort to conceal her irritation. He was determined to continue the hostility between them, it seemed. After their conversation at Merlin's Cavern the previous day, the barriers between them had seemed to diminish in the shared knowledge of the events of the past, yet now they were back in force.

'I just wondered if you'd found out anything about — well, what we were discussing yesterday,' she said.

'I'm going back to the office for some coffee. Join me?' He was already moving, and she kept in step with him. 'Actually, I haven't made any headway at all,' he answered her question as they left the greenhouse and headed towards the site office.

'Oh.'

'It is rather a delicate matter,' he said, noting her disappointment. 'It's not something you mention to everyone you meet.'

'Of course not,' Tansy murmured. 'Who have you mentioned it to, though?' She eyed him questioningly.

'Well, most of the people working here are too young to know anything about it,' he responded. 'There's old Joe, but he keeps a closed mouth at times.'

'Yes.' Tansy recalled her own efforts in that direction. She eyed Mark Harmon tentatively. 'So where do we go from here?'

'I don't know,' he confessed frankly. 'But there are one or two other people I can try yet. The child might not even be on the island any longer; had you thought of that?'

'Yes,' Tansy admitted. 'But I just have a feeling this is where the answer lies.

Actually — ' Changing the subject, she broached her main reason for coming down to the nurseries. 'I'm going into town this morning shopping and — well . . . '

'Meeting Tregarth?' he suggested calmly, when she paused.

Taken aback, she eyed him with surprise.

'I heard his helicopter going over last night,' he explained.

She was glad then that she hadn't tried to hide the fact that Tregarth had contacted her.

'As a matter of fact, I am having lunch with him.' She spoke almost defiantly.

They had reached the site office by now, and he opened the door for her to enter.

'Heather's going into town to deliver some floral arrangements at the civic hall,' he said unexpectedly. 'She'll be glad to give you a lift and direct you to wherever you're meeting Tregarth.'

His back to her, he was already

plugging in the kettle.

'Good.' Tansy smiled. 'It will give us a chance to have a chat.'

'About what?' Spooning coffee into two mugs, he turned and eyed her thoughtfully.

'Oh, nothing in particular,' Tansy responded, puzzled. 'I just thought that — well, I've hardly had a chance to talk to her.'

For a moment he was silent.

'I wouldn't waste your time trying to get her onto your side,' he said then.

'Onto my side?' Tansy eyed him angrily. 'What gives you the idea I need to get anyone onto my side?'

'It was just a thought,' he said. 'But even so, it would be pointless, don't you think, for you to get too involved with the employees here, if you're going to sell out to Tregarth?'

'It isn't a foregone conclusion that I will sell to him,' Tansy was stung into saying.

'Oh?' His eyebrows arched. 'It's not too late too try and get into your good graces, then, and try to influence you not to sell?' There was mockery in his tone.

Putting down the cup he had just handed her, Tansy stood up, her eyes sparkling dangerously.

'I don't think there's much point in my staying any longer, do you?' she asked quietly.

'None at all,' he returned. 'Enjoy your lunch,' he added, as she opened the door and walked out.

Colour stained Tansy's cheeks as she made her way back to the Lodge. Had it been too much to expect civilized behaviour from him? He had made no secret of his opposition to her plans, yet she had a perfect right to sell the nurseries if that's what she wanted to do. From the start, he had tried to force her into doing what he wanted by exerting emotional pressure through the fears of the employees. Now, he was accusing her of using the same methods against him! She couldn't help heaving a sigh then. At the cavern yesterday, learning together the truth of what had happened between her grandfather and her parents had seemed to unite them, trigger off the beginnings of a tentative friendship between them, and she had sensed that, in the right circumstances, he could be a good friend. Yet this morning they were back to confrontation, by the look of it. And why had she allowed him to goad her into saying that about selling out not being a foregone conclusion? She had decided weeks ago to free herself from this unwanted inheritance as soon as she could. Obstacles had raised their heads in the form of the wild flower meadow and the tenants' cottages, but these could be ironed out quickly enough. There had been an inference from the start — which she had firmly resisted — that she was under some kind of obligation to her grandfather to keep the nurseries in the family. Whilst she had believed Benson Whitton to be responsible for her parents' troubles, the way ahead had been clear. Now, in view of the mitigating factors surrounding his refusal to help her father out of his financial difficulties, things were not so clear-cut. Living in his house, surrounded by his possessions, it seemed to Tansy that everything presented a silent reproach. Had Mark Harmon been justified in feeling she intended ingratiating herself with the employees, she wondered now? Wasn't there, perhaps, a twinge of guilt which made her want to justify her actions in their eyes, if she were honest with herself?

It was only minutes later that she heard the sound of the Land Rover drawing up outside the Lodge. Picking up her jacket and bag, she hurried out. Heather was waiting for her, a stiffly polite smile on her face, and Tansy had no need to wonder if Mark Harmon had told her the reason for Tansy's trip into town. Climbing into the passenger seat, she turned and eyed the stacks of plants in the rear.

'How lovely!' she exclaimed impulsively. 'Is it some special event?'

Heather nodded.

'There's a civic ball tomorrow. We do the flowers for all the main events on the island: the annual flower show, the mayor's reception, the Whitton Lodge Garden Party — '

'Whitton Lodge Garden Party?' Tansy eyed her curiously. 'I've heard nothing about that.'

'Oh, we've made no plans this year, what with your grandfather dying and everything.' Heather looked uncomfortable. 'I shouldn't have mentioned it.'

'Please,' Tansy urged. 'I'm interested. Tell me about it.'

'Well, it's held on the first Saturday in July in aid of local conservation.' Heather spoke reluctantly.

'But that would be this Saturday!' Tansy exclaimed. 'Why didn't it go ahead as usual?'

Heather shrugged. 'We didn't think you'd want to be bothered, in view of, well, you know . . . '

Tansy frowned. Why did everyone assume that she wasn't interested in any

114

aspect of the nurseries at all, just because it was about to change hands?

'It could have gone ahead,' she said now. 'I wouldn't have objected.'

'Well — ' Heather was obviously regretting her slip of the tongue. 'Where in the city do you live?' Deliberately, she changed the subject and Tansy took the hint. When she named the vicinity in which she lived, a smile lit up Heather's features.

'The college I attended is quite near there,' she exclaimed, adding quietly, 'The time I spent there was one of the happiest parts of my life.'

'You sound as if you'd have preferred to stay on the mainland.' Tansy eyed her thoughtfully.

'My uncle paid for my college training,' Heather murmured. 'I had to come back here, to help out with the nurseries.'

'Surely he wouldn't have held you under obligation?' Tansy asked.

'Nevertheless, I felt I ought to come back,' Heather told her.

But that's only part of it, isn't it, Tansy thought shrewdly. *The other part is Mark Harmon . . .*

'Mark tells me the wild flower meadow is mainly your work,' she commented.

'Oh — ' Heather made a dismissive gesture. 'It was my uncle's work; I just went along to hold the seed trays for him.'

'I'm sure it was more than that,' Tansy said warmly.

'It was his dream.' Heather spoke reminiscently, after a moment. 'I only helped him make it come true.'

Eyeing her, Tansy wondered whether she could venture a further question or two. The constraint which had existed between them since her arrival seemed to have lessened somewhat. Perhaps, she thought wryly, it's become obvious to Heather now that, so far as Mark Harmon is concerned, I'm no competition . . .

'That meadow was his pride and joy,' Heather said suddenly. 'We keep it as a memento to him, apart from its own value for conservation purposes. If anything should happen to it . . . '

Tansy looked away in irritation. How many times was she expected to reiterate her assurances that she would insist that Paul Tregarth kept the meadow intact? For a moment there was silence, then Tansy eyed the other girl tentatively.

'What was he like, my grandfather?' she asked. 'Really like, I mean.'

Heather considered. 'He could be stern, even abrupt at times. But he was absolutely fair,' she said at last.

Was he, Tansy wondered? Had he been fair when he had turned his back on her mother's plea for help all those years ago? Yet had she the right to judge him, in view of what she now knew about those events, any more than she had a right to judge her parents? No one had come out of the affair with credit.

'He was a wonderful man. I'm proud to be related to him,' Heather said suddenly.

It seemed to Tansy, listening, that there was an unspoken message in the words. *Whilst you, his only grand-child, never came near him . . . .* The less they talked about Benson Whitton the better. Tansy thought then. She had plenty of other things to occupy her mind. In the aftermath of Paul Tregarth's telephone call, she had forgotten her attempts to contact David Firth yesterday. Now, her mind went back to that. In the light of day, the uneasiness she had felt at her inability to reach him and then being cut off so abruptly when she had managed to make contact, seemed foolish. It had been due to a mix-up, a crossed line, nothing more. There had been no need to call him at all, the impulse to do so stemming from an unaccountable feeling of loneliness which had stolen over her, urging her to reach out to something familiar. Heather's less than gracious refusal of her offer of friendship, following so soon on Mark Harmon's curtness, had for a while left her with the strong feeling of being an outsider on this lovely island, in an obviously close-knit community. Now, she realized that it had been a fanciful mood, a melancholy one even, which had taken hold of her for a while, partly brought on by living alone in the gloomy Lodge. If she were to spend any length of time there, she would have alterations done. The thought surprised her. There was no chance that she would be spending any longer there than was necessary . . .

The town was coming into view now, and she eyed the approaching buildings with relief. The silence between herself and Heather, after their promising start, had lengthened.

'Where shall I drop you?' Heather glanced enquiringly at her.

'Anywhere will do,' Tansy told her. 'I want to do some shopping before my appointment.'

Slowing the Land Rover down, Heather

waited as Tansy stepped on to the pavement and shut the door behind her.

'Thanks.' She smiled up at the other woman.

'Don't let Mark bully you into keeping the nurseries on, if that's not what you want,' Heather said unexpectedly, staring down at her through the open window. 'Life will go on for us all, whoever's in charge.'

She drove away before Tansy could make a response, leaving her staring thoughtfully after her. What a surprising thing for her to say! Mark Harmon's assistant, by the look of it, did not share his love for the nurseries, or for Calanara itself. She had detected a wistful note in Heather's voice when talking about the time she had spent on the mainland. Only loyalty to Benson Whitton, it seemed, had brought her back at all. It wasn't surprising. Heather, by all accounts, was a talented horticulturist. She could have gone far if she hadn't chosen to bury herself on this tiny island. Remembering the impending meeting with Paul Tregarth, she made an effort to dismiss Heather Parker from her thoughts. Her shopping didn't take long, and she presented herself at the Smugglers' Retreat with time to spare. Even so, Paul Tregarth had arrived before her, rising to his feet and beckoning to her from the corner table as she entered the restaurant and looked uncertainly around.

'Mr Tregarth?' She eyed the tall, grey-haired man with interest as she reached the table and took his out-stretched hand in hers.

'Miss Forrester. We meet at last.'

Despite the warmth of his smile, there was a shrewdness in the eyes which appraised her. This was a man who would drive a hard bargain, was Tansy's instinctive thought. And she could see, in the first glance, why Mark Harmon would not like him. The immaculately cut suit, the gold of his tie-pin and cuff-links, all contributed to the overall image of a man who courted success. And there was a ruthlessness about him, too, which Tansy sensed even in those early minutes of their meeting. A waiter was hovering, and Paul Tregarth beckoned him over as Tansy sat down.

'How about a drink whilst we wait for our food?' He smiled briefly at her. 'Then we can get down to finalizing things.'

Listening, Tansy had the impression that he regarded this meeting as a mere formality, the matter already cut and dried and only the bare details left to be discussed. Why should that bother her? Finance was no problem; the lawyers could negotiate that side of things, once a tentative agreement had been reached. Yet there was a niggling feeling at the back of her mind.

'Mr Tregarth — ' She eyed him uncertainly after they had ordered. 'One or two things have been brought to my attention . . . '

'Please, go on,' he invited, when she paused.

She took a deep breath. 'Well, there's

the wild flower meadow, for a start. You know of its existence, I take it?' She eyed him questioningly.

'Of course; how could I not be aware of it?' he asked lightly. 'It's right next to my golf-course.'

Hearing him, Tansy was reminded of Mark Harmon's sarcastic words about Paul Tregarth's intentions towards the meadow. She bit her lip.

'I've assured Mr Harmon that we can come to an agreement to leave the meadow intact,' she said then.

'Oh?' There was a quizzical lift of the eyebrows, though his smile didn't waver. 'Mr Harmon,' he continued thoughtfully. 'A truculent young man, I recall. We've had our differences in the past.'

Tansy's expression was thoughtful. Even now, eyeing the man seated across from her, she refused to believe there was any foundation for Mark Harmon's assertion that Paul Tregarth was behind the protracted acts of vandalism the nurseries had suffered. A man like

Tregarth would not stoop to those methods, surely? He had freely admitted a moment ago that he and Mark Harmon did not see eye to eye, yet it was a far cry from mutual differences to deliberate harassment.

'I have, as you know, said that all your employees will be offered alternative jobs,' he was saying now.

Alternative jobs. That sounded as if he had no intention of keeping the nurseries going in their present form, Tansy thought. If he had intended that, he would have said something to the effect that their jobs would be safe with him. She had already been aware that he had, in all probability, other plans for the nurseries. Why should it bother her so much now, when before coming to the island it had seemed a sensible solution which was hardly her concern? Calanara was getting to her, she realized then, weaving its own particular spell of enchantment round her like invisible strands. What was it her mother had said in her letter; something about the island never letting her go, once she had come to it? And it was the first time, too, that anyone had referred to the employees of Whitton Lodge Nurseries as *her* employees. It filled her with an odd sensation. They were her employees, weren't they? She was the owner, if only temporarily, of the nurseries, and as such, whether she liked it or not, all those people were her responsibility. She recalled old Joe's words, said so confidently yesterday. *You're Mr Whitton's granddaughter. You won't do any-thing against us.* Laura Harmon had said it too, some days ago. They all looked to her to safeguard their interests.

'Mr Tregarth — ' She cut into his conversation, and he broke off, eyeing her enquiringly. 'You haven't given me an answer yet about the wild flower meadow. And there's something else. Several of my employees, I understand, live in tenants' cottages situated on

Whitton land. They're worried about the effect your acquisition of the property will have on that — '

'They needn't be,' he cut in, smiling. 'I know of the cottages. They'll be allowed to stay there, of course. Though I'm sure you'll understand that in due course, a more realistic rent will have to be applied. I am a businessman, after all. As for the wild flower meadow, we'll see what can be done.'

The rest of it was lost on Tansy. He wasn't going to give her the assurances she needed. In that moment she knew that Mark Harmon had been right all along about this man. Left to him, there would be no nurseries, no protection for people like Joe, no wild flower meadow. There was no way, she saw now, that she could force a commitment from him to retain things on compassionate grounds, because this man did not know the meaning of the word. And, once the land was his, he would be able to do what he liked with it. Tansy sighed. It seemed to her then that she had known all along — known and ignored the fact — that she could not sell the nurseries and all they stood for to this man. Once she had come here, allowed the island to touch her heart, names to become faces and people, her plan had been doomed. She could no longer use the excuse that it would be a good thing economically for the nurseries, absolve herself of responsibility for these people, tell herself they would all have jobs. Mark Harmon had won, after all. She owed it to her grandfather — a man she had never met, yet whom she felt she was coming to know more and more — to carry on where he had left off and keep the nurseries in the family. It was as if he were standing by her chair, urging her on, giving her strength, as she faced the man seated across from her now.

'I'm sorry, Mr Tregarth.' She spoke quietly to him. 'I'm afraid I've wasted your time. I've decided I can't sell the nurseries to you, after all.'

The silence which followed her words

was unnerving, yet now she had actually said it, all hesitancy left her. It was as if everything that had happened since coming to Calanara had been leading up to this, and now the decision was made, she felt as if a weight had been lifted from her. Paul Tregarth was staring at her as if she had gone mad.

'I beg your pardon?' he said at last.

'I've changed my mind,' Tansy repeated. 'I'm sorry but that's my decision.'

'And when did you decide that?' His voice had lost its cordiality and sounded cold to her ears. She could understand his anger. Yet she had not deliberately kept him dangling. She had really wanted to sell to him, offload the responsibility of the nurseries onto other shoulders. It had been with a feeling of dismay, mingled though it was with anticipation, that she had realized that she could not turn her back on the people at the nurseries. She was, after all, more like her grandfather than she had imagined.

'If it's a question of price, I'll meet your figure.' At her silence, Paul Tregarth had spoken again.

'It's not that.' Tansy spoke almost regretfully. 'I can't sell the nurseries to you, that's all there is to it.'

'It's the meadow, isn't it? That ridiculous bundle of weeds!' The veneer of politeness was stripped completely from his voice now, and he was openly sneering. 'The old man's senile fancy.'

With a shock, Tansy saw the man behind the mask of geniality. This was the man Mark Harmon knew, the man he had told her about, yet she had not believed him. The insult to her grandfather only served to strengthen her resolve. Paul Tregarth would not get his hands on Whitton Lodge Nurseries whilst it was in her power to prevent it. Standing up, she spoke icily.

'In the circumstances, I'm sure you won't expect me to stay for lunch, Mr Tregarth.'

'There's nothing I can say to change your mind?' he asked.

Shaking her head, Tansy turned to leave. She was walking away, when he left his seat and gripped her arm.

'You'll regret it,' he said curtly.

Tansy looked into the cold blue eyes and flinched from what she saw there. Yet she wasn't alone against him — and the thought was a comforting one. Mark Harmon would be right there by her side. Whatever else they found to argue about, they would be united in that.

Some time later, she stepped out of the taxi which had brought her back to the nurseries. As it drove off, she looked down at Gatehouse Cottage, undecided. Mark Harmon's car was parked by the gate; at this time of day he would be having his lunch. On impulse, she walked down the lane and knocked at the cottage door. Shivering in the stiff breeze, she waited. Mark himself answered the door, his brows drawing together in a frown as he saw who the caller was.

'I thought I should let you know as

quickly as possible.' Tansy didn't waste time in preliminaries. 'I've decided not to sell the nurseries to Tregarth.'

For a long moment he stared at her.

'You'd better come inside and have something to eat,' he said at last. 'I take it you didn't wait around for the food?'

Some time later, Tansy sat in the lounge, drinking coffee and eating the snack Laura had insisted on preparing for her. Both she and Mark had heard the story by now, and though they were obviously pleased, Tansy noted that there was no sign whatsoever of self-satisfaction or triumph from either of them. Nor had they pressed her to explain in more detail her decision not to sell, or say whether she had given any thought to future plans for the nurseries. Yet she was aware of the speculation in Mark Harmon's eyes as he regarded her, and she wasn't surprised by it. After her apparent determination to sell the nurseries, her sudden turnabout must have come as a surprise to him.

She was aware that some sort of explanation was called for, yet she wasn't sure herself what had been the deciding factor. It seemed, looking back, that it had been a gradual process, a reluctant acknowledgement of her family responsibilities; something which had crept up on her so stealthily she had been able to ignore its existence until that moment in the restaurant. Then she had come face to face with it, and the time for prevaricating was over. As Mark continued to eye her thoughtfully, she put down her cup.

'All right, I know you must be wondering what brought about my change of heart.' She eyed him steadily. 'To tell the truth, I don't know myself exactly what decided me. I suppose it just became obvious to me very quickly that Paul Tregarth would make no firm promises with regard to the meadow or to the cottages which Joe and the others are occupying. I doubt if he'd have honoured them, even if he had made any.'

'I tried to tell you that, if you recall,' Mark said drily.

'Only too well,' Tansy admitted. 'Anyway, it just came to me more and more that he wasn't the right person to take on the nurseries.'

'Can I take it from that you're not intending to take over yourself and that you're still looking for another buyer?' Mark asked.

'I hadn't thought that far ahead,' Tansy spoke vaguely. 'But yes, I suppose I will be looking for another buyer. Does that satisfy you — or do you still think I should take over the reins myself?'

'I've never said that,' he protested. 'What I was so much against was selling out to Tregarth, knowing what he'd do with the business.' He took a sip of his coffee. 'Under a caring owner, the nurseries would go on in their present form, and that's all I'm bothered about.'

It occurred to Tansy again that her taking over at the nurseries was not something he would exactly welcome. Why was that, she wondered? Was he afraid she would try to interfere in the running of things? He had been happy to work under her grandfather, who would have been anything but a figurehead, except perhaps in the later stages of his illness. Was it because she was a woman? She eyed him thoughtfully now.

'I don't suppose you'd know of anyone who would be interested in acquiring the business?' she asked hesitantly.

'Depends on the price,' he responded. 'Tregarth's the only one around here with the kind of money you'd be talking about. Although — ' He eyed her speculatively. 'A few of us here at the nurseries wouldn't turn down the chance of forming a workers' co-operative to run the place between us, if we could raise sufficient capital.'

'Oh?' Tansy eyed him questioningly. It was the first time he had mentioned such a thing. Could this have been a large part of his objection to Tregarth's acquiring the place, she wondered? Were his noble sentiments about keeping the nurseries just as they were a mask for his real ambition of taking over himself? She couldn't help wondering again if he had hoped Benson Whitton would bequeath the place to Heather. She was a distant relative and she shared his interest in the place. Aware that he was awaiting an answer from her, she shrugged.

'I'm sure we could come to an agreement which would be satisfactory to everyone,' she told him. 'Would you like me to speak to my solicitors about it?'

'It wouldn't do any harm,' he responded. 'Unless, that is, you decide to stay on yourself?'

The remark puzzled her. What was he implying? A moment ago, she'd had the distant impression that her staying would be the last thing he wanted. She decided to test him out.

'And if I do?' She spoke challengingly. 'How would you feel about that?'

'Quite happy, so long as you allowed me a free hand in the running of things, as your grandfather did,' he returned candidly. So it was what she'd thought earlier. Herself as an absentee owner with him in charge . . .

'Suppose I decided I wanted to take, shall we say, a more active part in the business?' She eyed him speculatively.

He frowned. 'Depends what you mean by that. If you were serious in your intentions, moved over here, took an interest in island life — '

'Play the lady of the manor, you mean?' she interrupted. 'Is that the role you have in mind for me? If I did move over here, it would be because I wanted to learn the business, not entertain the Ladies Guild to tea at the Lodge.'

An irritated expression crossed his face. 'All I'm saying is that there would be no room for two bosses; your grandfather recognized that fact and you'd have to do the same.'

She eyed him doubtfully. He had made his position clear enough. Stay if you like — *but keep out of my way.*

And she couldn't help a feeling of relief that staying on Calanara was the last thing she wanted to do . . .

'Don't think you've heard the last from Tregarth,' he said suddenly. 'He doesn't give up that easily. He's waited too long to get his hands on the nurseries to give up meekly.'

'Surely there's nothing he can do?' Tansy asked.

'Nothing legal, perhaps,' he responded.

'What does that mean?' Tansy spoke sharply.

'Only that he's been harassing us on and off for a long time now,' he informed her. 'We may get more. Still, who knows?' He shrugged. 'It didn't work with your grandfather; perhaps the fact that it won't work with you either will come home to him eventually and he'll leave us alone.'

Listening, Tansy was aware of a feeling of uneasiness and if it had been anyone else but Mark Harmon in charge of the nurseries, she would have

looked to the future with foreboding
. . . A thought struck her then.

'So there's no reason now why the
Whitton Lodge Garden Party shouldn't
take place, is there?' She eyed Mark
tentatively.

'Who told you about that?' He
sounded surprised.

'Heather let something slip about it
this morning,' she explained.

'Typical!' Laura entered the conversation, her eyes twinkling. 'Heather
hates to miss a chance to show off her
horticultural talents. But it's too late,
surely, to contemplate putting the
garden party back on again? And I
know the next few Saturdays after that
are pretty booked up with community
events.'

'How much work is involved for the
nurseries?' Tansy asked.

'Surprisingly little,' Mark admitted.
'We get an outside caterer for the food,
and various organizations set up stalls.
We supply the premises and the plants,
of course. Various people run things like

tombola. The garden party is a real money-spinner, actually.'

'Then we'll do it,' Tansy said firmly. 'And I will man the tombola personally.'

'Right.' Mark rose to his feet. 'I'll get back to the nurseries and let them know the thing's back on, in that case. Mother will know what to do about arranging the rest of it. I'll see you later.'

Giving his mother a swift kiss, he left the room. Laura's expression was pensive. 'It will be a rush to get things ready,' she murmured.

'Then the sooner we start, the better,' Tansy responded.

The next few days passed in a flurry of activity. Saturday dawned fine and clear. People were about early, as Tansy saw when she looked through the Lodge window on her way downstairs. The caterers had arrived and were setting up their equipment. She hurried to join Mark and his mother, anxious to do her share to make the event a success. Even now, she wasn't sure why it was so important that the garden party should go on. She only knew that as the new owner of the nurseries, she wanted everything to continue along the same lines as it had in her grandfather's time.

People were stringing lights in the trees for the dancing that would follow in the evening, and Tansy's eyes sparkled as she saw them. It looked like being a wonderful day. The nursery employees were arriving; among them Heather Parker, who studiously avoided Tansy's glance, making her wonder if the other girl regretted her candidness on the journey into town the other day. She was in conversation with Mark now and glancing at them, Tansy couldn't help but notice the closeness of their figures. She looked quickly away. It wasn't something she hadn't already been aware of.

By late morning, the scene was a hubbub of activity. Despite the short notice, the news of the garden party's being on again had spread, and people were thronging the grounds. Only then did Tansy get an idea of how important the event was in the island social calendar. The whole of the island's population seemed to have congregated in those few acres of ground. In charge of the tombola stall, she was enjoying herself, much to her surprise.

'Tansy, there's someone I want you to meet.' Coming to her side, Laura took her arm and drew her across to where an elderly couple stood within the shade of a chestnut tree. Eyeing them curiously, Tansy was conscious of a wariness in the woman's eyes; something she had seen before in the eyes of several of the islanders. She knew she was still regarded by many of them as an outsider; they tolerated her among them and withheld their judgement until she had proved herself to them. How many of them, she wondered, watched and waited to see how she would handle the heritage left to her by her grandfather? More than ever then, she knew she had done the right thing in not selling out to Paul Tregarth. She had heard nothing further from him since the day she had turned down his offer, and had begun to hope that he would accept her decision gracefully.

'This is Mr and Mrs Harold Parker, Heather's parents.' Laura was introducing her to the couple now.

'How do you do?' Smiling, she shook hands with each of them in turn.

'So you're my cousin's granddaughter.' Harold Parker was eyeing her with frank interest.

'That's right,' she responded. 'What do you think of the floral arrangements? Heather's responsible for most of them, as you probably know. You must be very proud of her.'

'She's extremely talented.' Mrs Parker spoke for the first time. 'I know Benson thought so, too.'

Tansy had a feeling the remark was meant to convey to her the fact that she was the outsider, not Heather. She had already detected veiled hostility in the woman. Ignoring it, she spoke pleasantly.

'Enjoy yourselves. I must hurry back to the tombola, so if you'll excuse me — '

She was aware of Laura's puzzled expression as she turned and left them, yet she wasn't prepared to spend more time with them. Though they had spoken cordially enough, there had been an atmosphere, an attitude of studied appraisal which had annoyed her. She was Benson Whitton's granddaughter, the rightful owner of the nurseries. If that did not please them, there was nothing she could do about it. But she would not be trotted out for inspection as if she were a prize filly! The feeling of antagonism persisted for some time, ruffling her outward composure.

'Tansy, have you seen Mark?' Laura was by her side some time later, looking distracted. 'The plant stall needs stocking up.'

'I thought I saw him going towards the greenhouses,' Tansy told her. 'I'll have a look, if you'll mind the stall for me.' About to move away, she turned and eyed Laura tentatively. 'I'm sorry if I seemed abrupt with the Parkers, Laura,' she murmured. 'It was just . . .' She gestured vaguely, wary of hurting the older woman by voicing her opinion of the couple.

'It's all right.' Laura touched her arm briefly. 'They were a little offhand, I know. Try to understand; they're very protective of Heather, and like a lot of other people on the island, they're wary of you until they know just what you plan for the nurseries.'

'I do understand,' Tansy said with a sigh. 'But I do wish people wouldn't regard me as some kind of monster. Anyway, I'll be back in a moment.'

Turning, she left the older woman. The greenhouse was quiet when she entered. Mark and Heather were standing at the far end. Unaware of her entrance, they were laughing and talking. Standing in the shadow of the door, waiting for them to notice her, Tansy was aware of a feeling of envy. They were at ease in each other's company in a way which made her feel suddenly excluded, a feeling which crystallized into certain knowledge of what was wrong with her as she saw Mark smiling down into Heather's eyes. Despite their antagonism and his earlier hostility towards her, she was attracted to Mark and it was something which she should never have allowed to develop. Watching him now with Heather, she could no longer deny it to herself. It was time she left the island, she knew that now. She had stayed too long, allowed feelings to develop within her which could only lead to misery. As the couple caught sight of her, she spoke unsteadily.

'Mark, your mother needs more plants for the stall.'

Turning, she hurried away before either of them could reply. Outside again, she was making her way across the clearing when she felt her arm being gripped.

'Tansy? Hold on a minute! It's me!'

At the sound of the familiar voice, she turned. Immaculately dressed and looking oddly out of place in these surroundings, David Firth was smiling down at her.

5

Tansy eyed David incredulously, everything else leaving her mind.

'You could say you're glad to see me,' he said wryly, when she continued to look at him in amazement.

'Sorry, David.' She made an effort to recover herself. 'Of course I'm glad to see you! It's just that it's such a surprise! You're the last person I expected to see at this moment.' She shook her head in bewilderment. 'What are you doing here? Why didn't you let me know you were coming?'

He shrugged. 'It was an impulse which I gave in to, and there wasn't time to let you know, if I hoped to catch the ferry. As for what I'm doing here, I wanted to see you. I thought you would have been back home before now.'

'Things are taking longer than expected,' Tansy explained.

'Oh? What about that guy you were selling to? Surely you could have got things sorted out between you by now?' David countered.

'Well, there were complications,' Tansy admitted.

His eyebrows rose. 'What complications? And what's going on here?' He gestured around. 'I would have thought the nursery staff would have been getting the place ready for whatever plans the new owner has for it; instead there seems to be some sort of event taking place — '

'It's the Whitton Lodge Garden Party,' Tansy explained. 'It's held every year in aid of local conservation.'

'My, my!' He spoke lightly, yet there was something in his eyes which belied his tone. 'You *have* involved yourself in the local scene, in what I imagined was a flying visit! Have you seen — who was it — Tregarth?'

'Yes, I've seen him,' Tansy confirmed. 'But we can't discuss things here, David.' She glanced around her, aware that people were eyeing them curiously. She was recalling, too, her attempts to contact David a few days ago. The matter had gone from her mind, she realized with surprise; other things — notably the garden party — claiming her attention. The last few days had passed quickly and she realized now just how immersed in the proceedings she had become, all thoughts of her life on the mainland pushed to the back of her mind. She had vaguely known she had to leave soon, but had postponed her decision until after the garden party. Now, David's unexpected appearance on Calanara brought it all crowding back.

'I tried to contact you. I think the wires were crossed or something,' she told him.

Taking her arm, he steered her in the direction of the trestle tables which comprised the refreshment area.

'Yes; I have to apologize for that,' he murmured. 'The fact is — well, it was an inconvenient moment . . .'

Tansy glanced at him, startled. So it

hadn't been a mix-up, after all!

'You hung up on me?' she asked.

He made an apologetic gesture.

'Tansy, things have been happening in the city, whilst you've been rusticating here — '

'I *am* on leave!' She pulled away from him, annoyed. 'What's been happening? And why did you hang up on me like that?'

He took his time in answering, avoiding looking at her.

'Mike Hollingworth's getting ideas,' he said at last. Steering her to a seat, he sat down opposite her and looked around him, evidently expecting to be approached by a waitress.

'You have to serve yourself,' Tansy murmured abstractedly. 'I can't stay long, David. I'm running the tombola stall — '

'Tombola?' He eyed her quizzically, and she looked away uncomfortably. 'It's a charity function, David,' she pointed out.

'Hm. Well then — ' Shrugging

philosophically, he went in search of refreshments and Tansy sat in a fever of impatience until he returned with two cups of coffee.

'What ideas is Mike Hollingworth getting?' she asked, as he set the cups down on the table. Mention of her boss at the agency had made her uneasy. There wasn't a lot of love lost between the two of them. A shrewd business-man, there were times when his methods had caused her more than a small amount of concern. David seemed to be hesitating.

'He wants you off the Loder account,' he said at last.

'Wants me off? But why?' Tansy eyed him blankly. 'I've handled it well, so far.'

'I know you have,' David agreed. 'But you know how he is about giving the more important accounts to men.'

Tansy knew well enough. It had taken a fair amount of persuasion on her part for Mike to have trusted her with the account in the first place, yet she had more than justified that trust. Colour flamed into her cheeks now. So he had waited until her back was turned, then done this!

'Why?' She eyed David helplessly.

'We both know the kind of man he is,' David murmured. 'He's never pretended to be an angel.'

That was true, she acknowledged. Working for Mike Hollingworth meant being on your guard every moment of the day. Several times, she had considered looking for another job, yet had done nothing about it.

'What reason does he give for taking the account away from me?' she asked now in genuine bewilderment. 'And what has it to do with your avoiding speaking to me — ' She stopped as a suspicion dawned inside her; confirmed by the way David would not meet her eyes. 'He's giving the account to you, is that it?' she asked quietly.

'He hasn't actually given it to anyone yet.' David's tone was evasive. 'Just dropped hints like sledgehammers. But

I am the most likely person to take it on — that's true. I have been keeping an eye on it whilst you've been away, after all.'

Tansy looked away. So this was what lay behind her apparent inability to contact him the other day!

'And would you take it, David?' she asked at last.

He sighed. 'If I don't, he'll only give it to someone else,' he argued. 'Look, Tansy — ' Reaching across the table, he took her hand in his, eyeing her compellingly. 'I've been in a dilemma, wondering what to do for the best. That's why I didn't want to speak to you until I'd had time to think things out.'

'And now that you have thought things out.' Tansy moved her hand away from his. 'You're going to stab me in the back?'

David looked annoyed. 'I've just explained; he's definitely moving towards taking the account from you. What difference does it make who ends up with it?'

All the difference in the world, Tansy thought painfully, if someone who I thought was my friend accepts something which rightfully belongs to me . . .

'He can't take the account from me,' she said at last. 'Not unless I've made a mess of it.'

'He's the boss,' David reminded her. 'He can do what he likes.'

Tansy looked away from him. She felt suddenly as if the ground had been pulled from under her feet. And what hurt most was David's betrayal of her — for that's what it would be, despite his attempt to excuse himself. He'd always had the knack of justifying his actions, she recalled, though in the past it had always been tempered by that charm of his. Yet it was a charm which seemed suddenly shabby now . . .
Obviously sensing her thoughts, he spoke cajolingly.

'Come on, Tansy. I came here to warn you, after all; that surely counts in my favour! You need to get back to the office and quickly. Hollingworth's made no definite move yet, more sounding out and making veiled hints. But there's no time to lose. There doesn't appear to be a sailing on Sunday, so we need to be on tonight's ferry. Can you be ready to leave that quickly?'

Tansy acknowledged to herself that she could. The question was — did she want to? Was it worth fighting for, a job on those terms? It had always been difficult, working for Mike Hollingworth, yet it had been a challenge she had met with enthusiasm. Now, in the face of his unfair treatment, she had no stomach for it and the reason was obvious. She knew Mike Hollingorth for what he was; a man with few illusions and even fewer ethics. But she had thought of David as a friend, and it seemed now that friendship meant nothing, when placed beside ambition. He had come to warn her, it was true, and as he said, the account would go to someone else, if he refused it. Yet, in his place, she would have refused it out of hand; made her position clear even before the offer was made, and told Mike Hollingworth in no uncertain terms what she thought of his deviousness.

'He could be waiting until you come back before making a move,' David urged. 'And he won't do anything over the week-end. If you're in the office on Monday morning . . . '

Tansy nodded. Now that the shock of David's news was receding, anger was taking over. Of course she had to go back and fight for what was hers; she owed it to herself to do that. For a moment, she had a wild desire to run up to the Lodge, pack everything quickly and get back to the mainland to face her boss. Yet, just as quickly, the impulse faded. She couldn't walk out on the garden party so abruptly.

'Tansy?' David was eyeing her questioningly. 'Are we leaving?'

She shook her head. 'I can't go just yet. I can't let the people here down.'

'They managed well enough before

you came.' There was a cynical note in David's voice. 'I think it's a good thing I did come; this place seems to be putting a spell on you!'

Tansy had to acknowledge the truth of that. There was something here which called to her. And the people were beginning to accept her. Even Heather's attitude towards her had thawed. There was an honesty about the islanders which was at variance with David's own peculiar code; even Mark Harmon, who had been opposed to her plans from the start, had been open about his feelings. David was obviously aware of her thoughts and annoyed by them.

'I thought you'd appreciate my coming all this way to let you know what was going on back home,' he said.

'You could have let me know when I telephoned — twice — a few days ago,' Tansy pointed out. 'If you really cared, you'd have had no need to think things over.' Her voice shook. 'Anyway, I can't

leave now; not today. Monday, perhaps — '

'Monday might be too late,' David
interrupted tersely.

'Then you'll profit by that, won't
you?' She eyed him stonily. 'You've
come here and I appreciate it, but if
you're honest, it was only to clear your
conscience, wasn't it?'

David's mouth had set in a tight line.
'Okay, I — '

'Excuse me for interrupting.' Mark
Harmon's voice sounded behind Tansy
and she turned to find he had come on
the scene without either David or
herself noticing. 'They're about to
judge the children's pet competition
and my mother suggested you might
care to sit in on the judging panel,
Tansy.'

'Oh.' Surprised, she felt a surge of
pleasure go through her. 'I'd love to.
Mark, this is a friend and colleague
of mine, David Firth. David, Mark
Harmon.'

'How do you do.' Mark's tone held

studied politeness.

David inclined his head brusquely, barely observing the minimum rules of social politeness, before turning his attention back to Tansy immediately.

'I'll be on the ferry tonight, Tansy. I'll see you there, if you can manage to shake the straw off your shoes and get yourself off this oversized meadow you call an island.'

Tansy was aware of a feeling of shock. She had never heard David speak in such derisory terms before, and she sensed it had been done deliberately, to draw attention, perhaps, to the difference between Calanara and the mainland.

'Perhaps if you took the time to look round Calanara, you'd see it's a little more than that,' Mark said pleasantly. 'It's a fertile region with a thriving community — '

'Spare me the guided tour!' David snapped.

The two men eyed each other with undisguised hostility.

'You're welcome to stay for the remainder of the garden party.' Tansy spoke quickly, anxious to avoid a confrontation between them. 'But if you'd rather not, I'll understand.'

'I've seen as much of this place as I want to!' David responded. 'I'll see you later at the ferry terminal. Be there, Tansy — for your own sake!'

'Well!' Mark's tone was reflective, as he watched David's tall figure heading for the gates. 'What was all that about?'

'He's angry because I won't leave with him.' Tansy wondered why she was making excuses for David. 'There's a problem at the office.'

'Why aren't you leaving with him, in that case?' Mark looked down at her.

Tansy shrugged. 'I can't just walk out . . . '

There was a flicker of something indefinable in Mark's eyes for a moment.

'Then forget it for now,' he said quietly. 'The kids are waiting. Don't pick young Sally's gerbil again, that's all I ask. She's won three times already and we'll have a riot on our hands if someone else doesn't get a look-in this year!'

His matter-of-fact tone had a soothing effect on Tansy, and she allowed herself to be led over to the tent where the pet show was being staged. Yet her thoughts remained with David for quite a while afterwards. She couldn't help contrasting his self-seeking with Mark Harmon's dogged loyalty to her grandfather, even in death. Her mind was filled with anxiety for the future, along with anger towards Mike Hollingworth. How typical of him to have treated her like this, in her absence! David was right in one respect; she needed to be back on the mainland as soon as possible, to defend herself against her employer's tactics. She couldn't afford to wait until Monday, either. After the open-air dancing which would round off the day, she would need to be on that ferry. Her solicitors could take over the negotiations with interested parties and once she had mentioned Mark Harmon's suggestion of a workers' co-operative, she could forget Calanara. She had done what they wanted; refused to sell out to Paul Tregarth. How much further was she expected to involve herself in the nurseries' activities? She had her own life back on the mainland. The feeling was growing in her that the longer she stayed, the less she would want to leave. And what would be the point of that? She didn't belong here. What had begun as a flying visit had turned into an interlude; pleasant, but nevertheless as far removed from her own life as it was possible to be. She had instinctively liked most of the people with whom she had come into contact; with others, such as Mark Harmon, the feeling had taken longer to grow. Watching him now, head bent in concentration as he listened gravely to a little girl's confidences about her pet, Tansy acknowledged that so far as he was concerned, it was a feeling which could only grow, bringing heartache with it, if she stayed. A vague feeling at first, it had crystallized into more tangible terms when she had stood by the greenhouse door and seen the closeness between him and Heather. David's interruption had pushed the feeling to the back of her mind, yet now it returned to disturb her. They had seemed so content together — and she had been unprepared for her own reaction to witnessing the scene. Now, she wondered if more good than she'd at first envisaged had come out of David's arrival on the island; even if there had not been the subsequent urgency to return to her office, it had served to remind her that she did not belong here.

The rest of the afternoon passed in a flurry of activity, giving her no time, thankfully, to dwell on her problems. Later, she changed for the dance, managing to pack her clothes so that she could leave quickly, once she had put in an appearance. By seven o'clock, people were arriving, among them Heather and her parents. Mark had gone to greet them and his laughter, mingling with Heather's, only depressed Tansy further. Music was playing softly now, people drifting onto the floor to dance, among them Mark and Heather. When Mark asked her to dance later, she couldn't help wondering if the invitation had been made out of politeness, rather than a particular desire to dance with her.

'This is lovely,' she commented, glancing round. 'It must be the social event of the year.'

'Hardly,' he responded. 'Though I think everyone enjoys themselves. As well as the affair making money for the conservation society, that is. No, the battle of the flowers in August is where we really let our hair down. But you won't be here for that, will you?' He eyed her speculatively.

'No.' She shook her head. 'Your mother's told you I've decided to leave tonight after all, hasn't she?'

'She has.' His tone was thoughtful. 'It's rather sudden, though, after your earlier reluctance. You said something about a problem at the office. Is that why you're dashing off?'

She nodded, glad of a chance to explain her abrupt departure.

'My boss at the agency is trying to take one of my accounts from me and give it to someone else,' she admitted now. 'I've worked hard on it and I'm not going to stand by and let him do this to me.'

'I should think not,' Mark returned. 'Who is he planning to give it to, by the way?'

The question took Tansy by surprise. What could it matter to him — he knew none of her colleagues except David. Or had he realized that was where the problem was? Looking up at him, she saw the suspicion in his eyes.

'It's him, isn't it?' he asked softly, when she didn't immediately reply.

Miserably, she nodded. For a moment he didn't speak, yet his arm, holding her as they danced, seemed to tighten for a moment and she was aware of sympathy in his eyes, mingled fleetingly with anger.

'He came to warn me to get back quickly,' she said then.

'Don't try to defend him,' he responded curtly. 'He came to smooth the way; convince you that his taking over this account was inevitable.'

Tansy eyed him in surprise. It was only what she herself had accused David of, yet Mark's perception of the situation on such short acquaintance was unexpected.

'He would be the most likely person to take over the account,' she told him. 'He's been keeping an eye on things for me.'

'You're very trusting, you know that?' Mark was eyeing her oddly. 'Not just in this particular instance. You believed implicitly what your parents told you and condemned your grandfather without even hearing his side of things.'

'I was wrong,' Tansy acknowledged. 'I ought to have known there would be more to it than there appeared to be. Perhaps I just didn't dare allow myself to start thinking along those lines.'

'If you had, you'd have come to the island sooner,' Mark said. 'Now you're leaving again. Will you be coming back, once you've sorted things out?'

Tansy shook her head. 'There's no reason for me to come back,' she said quietly.

For a moment he was silent, though Tansy was aware again of his arm tightening around her.

'Perhaps you haven't looked hard enough for one,' he said at last.

What did he mean by that, Tansy wondered? Looking at him, she tried to read his expression. Had it been something to say out of convention, or had there been more behind it? What reason could there be for her to return to Calanara? She wasn't part of the life here; she was an outsider. Yet, she saw with sudden perception, she had more in common with the people here than she had with David Firth and others like him. The islanders were slow to accept newcomers but once they did, their loyalty and friendship never faltered.

'There's your quest for your half-brother or -sister, for one thing,' Mark said suddenly. 'I'm sorry I got no further with that, by the way. I seem to have come up against a brick wall.' He eyed her curiously. 'Don't you want to solve that little mystery?'

'Of course I do,' Tansy told him. 'But I just don't know where to start. If my father's name was put on the birth certificate, I can perhaps trace it back, once I'm on the mainland again.'

'*If* it was put on,' Mark murmured. 'He turned his back on the girl, don't forget. I wouldn't be surprised to learn that Benson Whitton persuaded her to leave his name off the official record. And without that, we're groping in the dark. Someone, somewhere on this island, knows where that child went,' he continued thoughtfully. 'But it will take time to find them.'

Time was something Tansy hadn't got.

'I will let you know if I find out anything,' he said now, looking down at her. 'I promise you that, whatever happens about the nurseries.'

'I know you will,' Tansy surprised herself by saying.

The dance was ending now. Mark guided her towards the clearing where Harold Parker and his wife were seated. Heather herself was engrossed in conversation with Laura some yards away, yet seemingly unconcerned, Mark lingered by Tansy's side.

'This is nice, isn't it?' Harold Parker smiled in Tansy's direction and she made an effort to be cordial.

'And to think it was all done at the last minute,' his wife commented. 'Mark and Heather have really worked hard at this.' Tansy couldn't help feeling that the woman's grouping of Mark and Heather together, with the exclusion of herself and Laura, despite their efforts, was deliberate.

'Yes, haven't they?' she murmured pleasantly. She had already sensed the other woman's dislike of her at their earlier meeting. Support came unexpectedly from Mark.

'Miss Forrester has worked harder than anyone to make the garden party a success.' There was a hint of reproof in his voice. 'Incidentally, the tombola stall she ran exceeded our highest expectations this afternoon. Everyone wanted to get a close look at her.'

'And why not?' Harold Parker put in gallantly. 'She's a most attractive lady.'

Tansy sent him a grateful look. After his wife's thinly veiled hostility, his comments were a welcome boost to her flagging morale.

Heather was approaching them now and Mark eyed her enquiringly.

'Dance, Heather? If you'll excuse us, that is, Tansy.'

'Go ahead.' She forced a smile. He had, after all, only been fulfilling his obligations to her by dancing with her. She watched as he and Heather made their way onto the floor.

'They look so right together, don't they?' Mrs Parker murmured.

Tansy ignored her, wishing Mark hadn't left her here with the couple. She would endure the woman's subtle malice for only as long as politeness demanded, before making her excuses and moving away.

'She's so talented.' The voice was relentless. 'Apart from her horticultural expertise, I mean. She's an artist; we have several of her sketches on the walls at home. Perhaps you'll have time to come and see them before you leave, Miss Forrester.'

About to decline, Tansy caught Harold Parker's apologetic glance. He could hardly have failed to be aware of his wife's deliberate attempt to discomfit her. She smiled reassuringly at him in acknowledgement. Heaven knew it wasn't his fault.

'Everyone's expecting an announcement about Mark and Heather soon,' his wife added smugly.

Tansy gritted her teeth, her patience eroding. Normally, she would have had no difficulty in ignoring the woman, yet it had been a long day with its fair share of traumas, and she was in no mood for the woman's subtle inferences. She was only too aware of the situation, in any case. Watching, it seemed to her that Mark and Heather were dancing closer than was strictly necessary. Yet what had it to do with her? He had made his opinion of herself obvious enough. True, the hostility he had shown towards her seemed to have disappeared, but to him she was just the boss. And the knowledge was suddenly, stupidly, painful. Nor was she prepared for the misery invading her mind now at the sight of Mark and Heather so obviously close. Why had she allowed these ridiculous feelings to develop, she wondered wretchedly?

'Benson thought highly of her, too.' Mrs Parker was speaking again.

Doesn't she ever give up, Tansy thought in irritation? What was the point in needling her like this? The situation was plain enough. Turning, she spoke more sharply than she had intended to the other woman.

'I do understand, Mrs Parker. Heather is a marvel in every way. And you needn't worry, my relationship with Mark is strictly business.'

The woman looked startled. 'I was merely trying to — '

'I know what you were trying to do,' Tansy interrupted. Anger was taking hold of her now; foolish, unreasoning anger, making her reckless. 'You've made your opinion abundantly clear. Without Heather, the business would have folded up years ago. What a pity my grandfather didn't leave it to her instead of me. But that's something you can't do anything about, I'm afraid.' She stopped, wishing she hadn't allowed herself to be goaded into saying all that. To her own ears, it had sounded petulant and smug, and she was aware of a feeling of shame. She should have been able to rise above this woman's spite, and seen the fear and insecurity which motivated it. 'I'm sorry,' she murmured. 'I shouldn't have said that.'

She looked round for an escape. In her anxiety about her job and misery at the sight of Mark and Heather together and so obviously content in each other's company, she was losing control of herself, saying things she instantly regretted. Glancing at Mrs Parker, she saw that the older woman's face was suffused with angry colour.

Reaching out, she gripped Tansy's arm. 'Yes, it is a pity he didn't leave the place to Heather; she deserved it!' she spat out. 'After the way your parents treated her, left her with nothing! And now, you, *his* daughter — trying to take her man away from her — '

'Maud!' Harold Parker's interruption was urgent. 'That's enough!'

She did not need him to tell her that. The anger left as suddenly as it had come, to be replaced by wariness. Tansy was staring at her, trying to understand the meaning behind her words. Something was pushing itself to the forefront of her mind, something she couldn't quite grasp. What had her parents to do with Heather? What had Mrs Parker meant, when she'd said they had left her with nothing? They wouldn't even have known her; she'd have been just a baby at the time Tansy's parents were on the island, if she had been born at all.

'Mrs Parker — ' She spoke unsteadily, reaching out to touch the other woman's arm. 'I'm sorry I said what I did; please forgive me. I'm not trying to harm Heather in any way . . .'

There was relief in the other woman's eyes now and for a moment Tansy was puzzled by it.

'Please don't apologize; it was wrong of me to say what I did.'

There was no mistaking the other woman's agitation. Does she think I'll hold Heather responsible, take my spite out on her because her mother spoke out of turn, Tansy wondered incredulously? Harold Parker was eyeing her now, and the wariness she had seen before in his wife's eyes was mirrored in his. Why? Surely they didn't regard her as that much of an ogre? And why had Mrs Parker backed down so quickly? It was obvious that she regretted her outburst, yet there was more to it, Tansy sensed. She cast her mind back, trying to recall exactly what the other woman had said. *His* daughter; that was how she had referred to Tansy. Why did this woman hate her father so much? There had been more than scorn in her voice; there had been signs of a deep bitterness etched into the other woman's mind so deeply that it seemed the passing of time had done nothing to soften it. What had Tansy's father done to make her feel like that? Tansy drew in her breath sharply then, wondering for a moment if Maud Parker could be the woman her father had abandoned all those years ago. Was it possible? She discarded the idea immediately. The woman had gone abroad; married there, according to what Tansy's own mother had said in her letter. Surely she would never have returned after abandoning her child so callously? Then the other woman's meaning was taking effect and the whole thing was clicking into place. Heather — so near herself in age; her only just disclosed talent for art. Tansy looked towards the dance-floor then, sought out Heather and Mark. The other woman was laughing, her head close to Mark's shoulder now, and as she looked, Tansy knew the truth at last; knew and wondered how she had managed to miss the connection before. It was all so clear, suddenly. The Parkers — Benson Whitton's cousins; the childless couple, now the elderly parents. And it explained Mrs Parker's hostility towards herself. There could be only one conclusion to be drawn and if Tansy had been in any doubt at all, the expression on Harold Parker's face now would have dispelled it instantly. The baby her father had abandoned all those years ago was right here, under her nose. Heather Parker, the woman who had been introduced to Tansy as a distant cousin, was, in fact, much more closely related to her than that. She was her half-sister . . .

6

'Heather's the one, isn't she?' Tansy spoke unsteadily. 'That baby of my father's; it was Heather, wasn't it?'

'No! You're wrong — ' Maud Parker made an ineffectual attempt to rectify the damage her vindictiveness had caused, but it was too late and she knew it. Turning, she looked with stricken eyes at her husband, who gazed back helplessly at her. Tansy stared at Heather, still hardly able to comprehend the sudden turn of events. She had not for a moment dreamed that the baby she was so anxious to trace had been so close to her, all the time. And yet, in hindsight, how could she have missed it? Her grandfather would have chosen people he felt he could trust with the baby; people, possibly, who were unable to have a child themselves.

'Please; she doesn't know ... '

Harold Parker had gripped her arm entreatingly, and she turned to look at him.

'It *is* true, then?' she asked shakily. 'Heather is the one?'

He nodded reluctantly. 'We've brought her up as our child,' he muttered. 'We never thought anyone would find out.' He cast a reproachful glance at his wife.

'Why didn't you tell her?' Tansy eyed him incredulously. 'You might have known it would come out, sooner or later! And she had a right to know.'

'Benson made us promise not to tell her — '

'He was wrong!' Tansy interrupted fiercely. 'You were all wrong!'

Even now, the revelations of the last few moments were still sending shock waves through her. Heather Parker — her half-sister! It was all so easy to understand now. Benson Whitton's generosity towards Heather, educating her, sending her to the best horticultural college he could find, once it was seen she had a talent for that sort of work, had not just been the kind-hearted gesture of a relative or even an employer. He had taken on responsibility for the baby even before its birth and it was a responsibility which he had not relinquished over the years. Tansy shook her head helplessly. So her quest to find her half-brother or -sister had ended so quickly and unexpectedly, on the eve of her departure from the island! She had an overpowering desire then to run across the dance-floor to Heather and tell her the whole story. Yet she held herself back. It would be as much of a shock to Heather as it had been to her and needed to be handled carefully. She scanned the other woman's face eagerly now for a trace of the father they had shared, absurdly disappointed when she found none.

Maud Parker had turned and left with Tansy hardly being aware of the fact, her anxious husband in her wake. Tansy continued to stare at Heather, laughing now at something Mark had said. Her thoughts were agonized. She had to tell her; somehow, she had to let Heather know- ... The music had stopped. Tansy heard Laura call out to Heather, who turned and headed in her direction. About to follow, Mark looked across at Tansy, noting that she was now alone. After escorting Heather to his mother's side, he made his way across to Tansy. Watching his approach, she resisted the urge to go and meet him, forcing herself to calmness.

'Mark — ' She spoke breathlessly when he reached her side, and he looked at her in concern.

'What's wrong? You look as if you've seen a ghost!'

She almost smiled at his choice of words. 'Mark — ' She touched a fluttering hand to her cheek in an effort to restrain her excitement. 'I must talk to you.'

'All right; talk,' he invited, seating himself beside her.

'No, not here — '

Leaving her chair, she moved towards the trees at the edge of the clearing and he followed.

'This is getting very mysterious,' he commented, eyeing her questioningly, as they reached the shelter of a glade some yards from the dancing.

'Mark — ' She stared up at him, her eyes feverish with excitement now. 'The baby — my half-sister — it's Heather!'

'Heather?' He eyed her incredulously. 'How did you come to that conclusion?'

'Her mother let something slip and when I challenged the couple, they admitted it,' Tansy confessed unsteadily. 'When you think about it, it all makes sense. She's around my age, and the Parkers are an elderly couple, cousins of my grandfather's. What was more natural than that he'd put the child with them? They live over the other side of the island, well away from the nursery, where people might not have heard about the scandal.'

'I can hardly believe it,' Mark muttered. 'Are you sure the Parkers understood what you were saying?'

'Quite sure,' Tansy told him.

'Then why let her come and work

here, if he'd gone to all that trouble to get her away?' he asked.

'I don't know,' Tansy said frankly. 'Unless he felt it was safe, once her mother had left.'

Mark frowned. 'She did show her talent for horticulture at an early age, I understand,' he murmured. 'It would have looked odd if he'd tried to prevent her from taking up a career in the family nurseries. Okay.' He nodded briskly. 'Assuming you're right, what do you propose to do about it?'

'Well, she has to be told the truth,' Tansy responded.

'No.' His voice had a sharpness in it. 'You can't just go and break that kind of news to her. Obviously, she's never been told about her true background.'

'But someone has to tell her!' Tansy protested. 'Preferably, Mr and Mrs Parker. But I doubt if they'll be willing, since they've kept it a secret all these years. She has to know, Mark!' She eyed him entreatingly.

'Look — ' Drawing a hand through

his hair, he sighed. 'I understand how you feel, believe me! But this needs to be handled with care. Have you any idea what it will do to Heather, finding out she's not Benson Whitton's relative, after all? She doted on him; it would shatter her if she found out.'

'She has a right to know who her parents really were,' Tansy insisted. 'And she would want to, I'm sure of that. I'd want to know — wouldn't you?' Her voice shook a little. 'I can't undo what my parents did to her but I can try to make it up to her at least.'

'It's not your debt, Tansy!' Mark eyed her in exasperation. 'You can't carry your parents' mistakes on your shoulders! Forget it.'

'I find my sister — and you want me to forget it?' Tansy asked in a choked voice.

'Listen to me!' Taking her by the shoulders, he eyed her compellingly. 'I've known Heather since we were both kids. I know exactly how she'll feel, finding out Benson Whitton and she weren't related, as she thought.' His voice grew gentler. 'I know how you feel, too. But this isn't the moment for disclosures of that sort. This needs to be handled tactfully.'

'Mark, Heather is my half-sister!' Tansy cut in desperately. 'Why does everyone seem to think she won't feel the same way as I do about it? We've so much to give to each other — ' She broke off as she heard Mark's low exclamation. His gaze had gone to the edge of the clearing. Turning, she saw Heather standing there. The horror on her face was thrust into sharp relief by the glow of the light strung in the tree behind her. She was white, glassy-eyed with shock, and it was obvious that she had overheard most of their conversation.

'Heather — ' Mark moved instinctively in her direction, yet before he could take a step, she had turned and darted out of sight. Thrusting a swift, exasperated glance over his shoulder at Tansy, he hurried after the other woman.

For a moment Tansy hesitated. All her instincts urged her to follow, to try and lessen the effect the sudden disclosure of Heather's real background must have had on her. She could imagine the other woman's state of mind, knowing how she herself had felt not long ago. Hurrying in Mark's wake, she reached the edge of the clearing. Both Mark and Heather were lost to view now. After some minutes' fruitless searching, she headed back to the dancing, hoping that Heather had made her way back there. There was no sign of her, nor of Mark. Catching sight of her, Laura Harmon beckoned and Tansy hurried across to her.

'Tansy? Is something wrong?' The older woman eyed her in concern as she reached her side.

'Oh, Laura!' There was a tremor in Tansy's voice. 'I've made a mess of things.'

'Nothing can be that bad.' Laura touched her arm briefly. 'Tell me about it.'

Tansy needed no further prompting to relate the events of the last few minutes.

Laura listened without comment until she had finished.

'I never meant for Heather to find out this way, Laura.' Tansy ended on a distressed note.

'What's done is done.' Laura's voice was gentle. 'And here's Mark now. Perhaps he'll know where Heather's gone to.'

Turning quickly, Tansy saw Mark striding across the clearing towards them, his expression grim.

'You haven't found her, then?' Tansy eyed him anxiously as he reached their side.

'No.' His tone was worried. 'I'm going to get the car and have a drive round, to see if I can spot her. I saw her parents leaving some minutes ago and she wasn't with them.'

'Oh, Mark.' Tansy's expression was contrite. 'I'd give anything to have avoided this — '

'It's a bit late for regrets,' he cut in. 'All we can do is try and keep the damage to a minimum. Once we've found her, that is.' Turning, he left them, threading his way through the dancers towards Gatehouse Cottage.

'I'm going to have a look round, too.' Tansy spoke determinedly. 'Where do you think she's most likely to head for, Laura? You know her as well as anyone.'

Laura shook her head, frowning. 'There's nowhere in particular I can think of — ' She broke off at the sight of Joe Traynor beckoning to her from a few yards away. 'Excuse me, Tansy.' Leaving her, Laura crossed over to the elderly man and they spoke urgently for a moment or so. Watching, Tansy saw Laura's eyes fill with horror. Hurrying across to them, she caught at Laura's arm.

'What is it; what's wrong — '

Laura turned agitated eyes towards her. 'It's the meadow; the wild flower meadow . . . '

Even as she spoke, people were running in that direction; others who had been dancing, stopping uncertainly as they realized something was amiss. There was no need for Tansy to ask further questions; already her nostrils were picking up the smell . . .

'Oh, no!' The words were wrung from her throat.

People were hurrying towards the greenhouse now, Joe and Laura among them, and Tansy lost no time in following. Reaching the top of the lane, she saw the ominous flickering reflected in the greenhouse windows and her mind filled with horror. That beautiful meadow — on fire! Reaching the spot, she stared with anguished eyes at the sight before her. The fire had obviously started near the gate and was spreading rapidly now through the top half of the meadow; away, she saw with relief, from the nursery buildings. The breeze wasn't strong, yet there was no doubt that the flames had taken a firm hold and the meadow would be destroyed if action wasn't taken immediately.

'Has someone called the fire-brigade?' She looked round anxiously at the onlookers.

'They're on their way,' a man told her.

Several people were running forward with buckets, yet the small amount of water they contained had little effect on the flames. Unable to do anything to help, Tansy could only stand watching helplessly, her ears strained for the sound of the fire-engine's siren. *Someone do something*, she thought desperately. One of the men had dragged forward a huge pipe which had been hurriedly fitted to the water-supply and she watched tensely as the contraption went into action. Several people were stamping out pockets of fire as best they could with their feet, others were beating desperately at the flames with pieces of sacking.

'Here, give me one of those — ' Unable to stand idly by any longer, Tansy snatched at a pile of sacks under the arm of a man hurrying past and followed him. The tightness of her dress, coupled with her high heels, made running difficult, yet she moved grimly on. Once inside the gate, she began to beat wildly at the flames, without success. The heat was intense; in seconds she was gasping, yet determinedly she continued her efforts.

'Here; give me that! Get back outside the gate!' It was Mark Harmon's voice behind her. Taking the sack from her, he propelled her firmly back outside the gate, where she stood irresolutely for a moment, watching as he turned back to the flames.

The distant sound of a siren caught her ears then, and her heart leaped in thankfulness. The smoke was in her nostrils, pricking her eyes and making them water, her face begrimed and her cheeks burning, yet she was hardly aware of any of it. The fire-engine was pulling up beside the greenhouses moments later, the crew moving quickly into action.

'Tansy, come away.' Laura took her arm, drawing her back to the cluster of watchers standing a little way off.

'All those beautiful flowers . . . ' Tansy's voice was cracked.

'We'll plant more,' the older woman said reassuringly. She looked at Tansy's dishevelled figure and shook her head.

'You shouldn't have gone in there,' she said chidingly.

'I had to do something.' Tansy spoke distractedly, her eyes still on the scene before her.

'They'll soon have things under control,' Laura comforted.

'I hope Mark's all right.' Tansy spoke unsteadily, having lost sight of him temporarily.

'He's all right. Look, he's coming away now,' Laura said.

Mark was leaving the meadow, turning towards the group of watchers. There was a slump to his shoulders and an air of defeat about him which caught at Tansy's heart. She knew how much the meadow meant to him — to all of them. Now, in the space of a few moments, it seemed as if it were all gone.

Reaching their side, he stood with them, watching as the firemen went about their work. His tie undone, his formerly immaculate suit and white shirt now smeared and blackened, he looked as dishevelled as Tansy did. No one spoke as the firemen fought to bring the blaze under control. Tansy watched miserably as a column of smoke spiralled upwards after the flames had been extinguished. It wasn't possible to see much through the haze, yet from the limited view she did have, it appeared that the meadow hadn't been totally destroyed. Still, it was bad enough. She looked up at Mark, the wretchedness in his eyes catching at her heart. He had been so proud when he had shown her that meadow not long ago . . . The vague feelings growing in her for him earlier were nothing compared to those which surged through her as she saw the hopelessness in his blackened face. Impulsively, she caught at his hand, speaking urgently.

'We can plant more, Mark; meadows and meadows more.'

For a moment he made no response, then he seemed to come out of a daze and looked back at her, squeezing wordlessly the fingers she had placed in his. Tears blinded Tansy's eyes at the simple gesture. Then the group around them was parting; someone was pushing through and Heather was beside them, her eyes anguished.

'Oh, Mark — '

Tears ran down her face unheeded as she reached his side and buried her head against his shoulder. Automatically, his arms went round her, Tansy's hand being released from his grasp. In her emotional state, it was like a slap in the face and she turned sharply away. There was no doubting the sincerity of Heather's emotion, coming on top of the shock she'd had earlier, and whilst Tansy felt no anger at her unwitting interruption, her heart ached as she watched them. What further proof did she need that Mark was in love with Heather, or that she herself was in love with him? His head bent towards Heather's now, he was speaking soothingly, as if to a child. Standing apart from them, she felt excluded and unwanted. What point had there been in trying to comfort him, she wondered? All the comfort he needed, he could get from Heather. She averted her face from them, unable for a moment to hide the pain she was feeling. Why, oh why, had her grandfather left her this legacy? It was a bitter legacy and one which she wished with all her heart she was free of. There was nothing for her here on Calanara.

Turning, she made her way through the group of onlookers, hardly aware of them. How could the fire have happened? She shook her head helplessly, tears pricking at her eyes. Yet it wasn't just the meadow's fate which caused them, but her own misery. The sight of Mark and Heather together, united in their sadness and apparently oblivious of her or anyone else, had only added to her pain.

'Tansy.'

Hearing Laura's voice, she turned to see the older woman following her.

'I'll walk with you. I've seen enough!' Her own face tear-streaked, Laura was having as much difficulty in controlling her emotions as Tansy. 'We have to think positively,' she murmured, taking Tansy's arm as she reached her side. 'At least none of the buildings was touched. Thank heavens the meadow is well away from them and that the wind was blowing in the other direction. It looks as if half the meadow has been destroyed; we'll know better how things are, tomorrow.'

Tansy's fingers, round Laura's arm, tightened for a moment. Together, they walked down the lane towards Gatehouse Cottage. Tansy followed the older woman inside, watching as she plugged in the kettle for tea.

'How did the fire start? Has anyone any idea?' she asked.

Laura sighed. 'The weather's been hot and dry for a while. Carelessness, perhaps . . . '

Something in her voice made Tansy look at her sharply, trying to read her expression.

'But country people are so careful; they know the dangers — ' She stopped then, her mind suddenly recalling what Laura had told her about sporadic acts of vandalism, and Mark's belief that the incidents were instigated by Paul Tregarth. Her head came up sharply and she drew in her breath. 'You surely don't think it's deliberate?'

It couldn't be! However angry he was by her refusal to sell out to him, Paul Tregarth couldn't intentionally destroy a meadow filled with rare wild flowers as an act of spite or an attempt to move things his way? She couldn't believe that; she wouldn't! It was a coincidence, nothing more, the fire following so quickly after her refusal to sell.

'We don't know; we can't start pointing the finger.' Laura spoke warningly. 'Don't go jumping to con-clusions, Tansy.'

Tansy eyed her shrewdly. 'But you think Tregarth's behind it, don't you?' she asked.

Laura sighed and gestured helplessly. 'My own feeling is that he probably had nothing to do with it,' she said at last. 'Though Mark will take some convincing of that, I think. But Tregarth is no fool; he'd know suspicion would fall on him, coming so soon after he'd spoken to you. No, he's not that stupid.' She shook her head. 'It's just a tragic accident,' she went on. 'We can prove nothing else — and I'm not sure I'd want to.' She gave a little shiver. 'Paul Tregarth is an aggressive neighbour — but a powerful enemy who won't stop at sabotage? I don't know. Any accusation by us would lead to confrontation. We've lived uneasily beside him for years; better that than open warfare, don't you think?'

'But if he is behind it — ' Tansy began.

'We'll know better in the morning. Perhaps the fire department can determine what started the fire. All we can do is wait.' Laura spoke tiredly. 'Mark will be taking Heather home; she's naturally very upset. The meadow was her pride and joy; she planted it for your grandfather years ago.'

Tansy nodded wretchedly. It had been a bad day for Heather; for all of them, in fact. The sooner it was over, the better.

Some time later, she made her way down to the Lodge. Sleep was elusive when she went to bed, her mind going over the events of the day. The garden party had been a resounding success; yet that success had been completely overshadowed by the day's tragic end. Had Tregarth caused the fire, or was it better, as Laura had intimated, not to think along those lines until and unless proof was produced that he had been behind it? Yet, accident or not, it was only a setback, she knew that. The meadow would bloom again; Mark would see to that, with Heather's help. It seemed there was no role for her to play here, no situation where she could help. Despite her own growing feelings for the island and the friendship most of its inhabitants had shown her, she felt more of an outsider at that moment than ever. All she seemed to have done since coming here was cause trouble. By her actions, she had destroyed Heather Parker's world, taken her family pride away from her and put nothing in its place, except the knowledge that she was the illegitimate daughter of parents who hadn't wanted her. No wonder she had run away, unable to cope with the knowledge.

Sighing, Tansy stirred restlessly in the bed. Would Heather, once the initial shock had worn off, be able to forgive her for telling her what others had thought best to conceal from her? Had they been wiser, after all? She didn't know. All she did know was that the sooner she was out of the lives of these people, the better it would be. Things would settle down for Mark and Heather once she had gone back to the mainland. Presumably they would marry at some point in the future. At least Heather had her love for Mark. She had not taken that away from her. Her own growing feelings for him she would stifle without mercy. She couldn't help thinking then that had her father been able to look into the future, he might have seen that one of his daughters would have to pay the price for his treatment of the other . . . Only when the telephone rang and she picked it up to hear David's voice, did she remember him, and his warning to be on the evening's ferry. The fire had driven it completely from her mind. It was too late now, and in any case, she could not have left, under the circumstances. She could only hope that Mike Hollingworth would make no move against her before Monday, and it was only then that she realized with surprise that she had unhesitatingly given preference to affairs on the island over her professional problems.

'So you decided not to come back home?' His clipped tones betrayed nothing of the anger she knew from experience he was feeling.

'David! I thought you'd have left — '

'The ferry's about to leave; I thought I'd just make sure you really knew what you were doing,' he interrupted tersely.

'I was intending to catch the ferry,' she told him. 'But — '

'Don't tell me; let me guess,' he interrupted. 'The child's gerbil died of shock when it didn't win first prize again this year and you felt you had to stay to comfort her. Or was it that you agreed to lend a hand with the parish jumble-sale or you forgot you'd arranged to go to a meeting of the ladies' sewing circle?'

Tansy's fingers tightened over the receiver. After the evening's events, this was something she could do without . . . She had hoped, too, that he would have cooled down by this time, at least enough for them to have a reasonably civilized conversation.

'It was none of those things, David!' she said at last. 'We had a fire.'

'Oh?' His tone held reluctant concern. 'Anyone hurt?'

'Fortunately, no.' Tansy told him. 'But my grandfather's wild flower meadow was partially destroyed.'

There was a short silence.

'You mean to say you missed the ferry because of a bundle of wild flowers?' he asked at last. 'You really are taking all this rather seriously, aren't you?'

'I couldn't have left them with it, David!' she protested. 'You can't imagine how upset we were — '

'We?' he echoed drily.

Tansy was silent. She couldn't help wondering what he would have said if she'd told him that all thoughts of leaving the island had completely gone from her mind in the wake of her discovery that Heather was her sister, even before the fire had occurred. He knew nothing of that business, she recalled now. And, she realized, she preferred things to stay that way for the moment.

'I'm sorry if you think I'm getting too involved in things here, David,' she said now. 'But I have a certain amount of responsibility to these people. Surely you can see that? Besides — ' Her voice cooled as she remembered his reason for coming to Calanara. ' — you're hardly in a position to start lecturing me about where my priorities lie.'

'You shouldn't have come to the island at all,' he said impatiently. 'You could have put the whole thing in the hands of your legal people, taken the money and forgotten about the blasted place!'

It was what he would have done, she knew. Perhaps he was right. If she hadn't come to Calanara, there would be no crisis with her job, no heartache from falling in love with a man who was committed to someone else and no disillusionment about the way her parents had behaved towards an innocent child. Would things have been the same between David and herself if she hadn't come, she wondered now? Sooner or later, she would probably have seen through the surface charm to the shallowness beyond, yet she would have viewed it more philosophically, not having a man like Mark Harmon against which to measure him.

'Are you there, Tansy? I'll have to go; the ferry's about to depart.' David's voice broke into her thoughts. 'Don't say I didn't warn you about what was going on, will you? I can't stop Mike Hollingworth doing what he wants to do.'

No, Tansy acknowledged. He had tried to warn her, at least. And she could see then the reason for his unusually strong anger at the fact that she wouldn't leave. He had wanted her to come back and tackle Mike Hollingworth or resign from the firm, thus saving him the necessity of making a decision which pricked at his conscience. Tansy sighed. Whatever happened now or in the future, she and David would be going their separate ways . . .

'Goodbye, David.' She spoke regretfully into the mouthpiece.

'I'll call you . . . ' His voice was faint. A moment later, she heard a click as the connection was broken.

Sighing, she lay back on her pillow, staring into the darkness, and it was a long time before she slept.

She was up early after a restless night, remembrance of the previous day's events flooding back immediately into her mind. She lost no time in making her way down to the meadow, the severe scorching becoming evident the nearer she came to the spot. Several people were moving about or standing by the gate, their expressions pensive, and she easily picked out Mark Harmon's tall figure amongst them. Catching sight of her, he broke off his conversation with his companion and made his way over to her. He looked tired, she noted, though the defeated stoop of his shoulders which had been so apparent the previous evening was gone.

'Any clues as to how it happened yet?' she asked as he reached her side.

'The firemen found spent matches near the gate,' he told her. 'Looks as if someone at the dance wandered out here and became careless.'

Tansy relaxed slightly. At least he wasn't accusing Paul Tregarth yet, and treating the matter with caution.

'So you think it was just an unfortunate accident?' she ventured.

'What proof is there that it was anything else?' he asked heavily. 'We had quite a few people here last night, a number of them town folk who aren't as aware of the dangers as country folk. But it's still careless.'

Tansy eyed him sympathetically. Though he was back in full control of himself, she knew how much the partial destruction of the meadow had affected him.

'We can re-plant,' she said quietly.

'True,' he acknowledged. 'But some of those seeds were rare and not easily obtained.'

Spotting a small cluster of white and silver flowers at the edge of the fence, miraculously untouched by the fire, Tansy stooped and picked one, holding it to her nostrils. Merlin's Tears, the island's own flower . . .

'Pity the old man wasn't around last night to watch over the meadow for us,' Mark remarked whimsically, his eyes on the flower she was holding.

Tansy was silent. She preferred to think he had been; and the survival of these flowers in the midst of the destruction was an omen for the future, a sign that the meadow would one day be restored to its former beauty.

'How is Heather this morning; have you seen her?' she asked.

'No, but we've spoken by telephone,' he responded. 'She seems a lot calmer.'

'Good.' Tansy looked away for a moment. 'I can't tell you how sorry I am about what happened,' she said then. 'It was a terrible way for her to have found out about her background.'

'Yes, it was,' Mark agreed. 'But it can't be helped and she seems to have accepted the situation now.' He hesitated, then continued, avoided her eyes, 'She doesn't want you contacting her just yet, if that's your intention.'

'Oh?' Hurt by his words, Tansy couldn't hide her dismay. 'I can understand how she would feel about our father, but surely she wouldn't extend that to me?'

'Nevertheless, that's the way she wants it, and we have to respect her wishes.' Mark's tone was firm. Noting Tansy's stricken expression, his voice softened. 'Give her time,' he urged. 'She was devoted to your grandfather. It was quite a shock to her, finding out he wasn't a blood relative, after all.'

Tansy nodded. Despite his good intentions, Benson Whitton had a lot to answer for, she couldn't help thinking. Not that it lessened her own father's guilt, but if Benson Whitton had not instructed the Parkers never to tell Heather the secret of her parentage, she might have been saved a lot of pain. He had assumed rights to which he was not entitled, in a misguided effort to protect Heather at some future time, yet it had all been to no avail. In the end, the truth had come out and Heather had been hurt anyway. Meanwhile, all she could do, as Mark had said, was accept Heather's decision and hope that in time she would come to feel differently. They were half-sisters, after all, and the mistakes of the past should not be perpetuated in the present. She had so much to share with this new-found sister, yet Mark was something they could never share. The thought reminded her of her decision, arrived at late last night, to leave the island as soon as possible.

'I'll be leaving tomorrow, Mark,' she told him now.

He frowned. 'I'd thought — after all this . . . ' He gestured towards the meadow. ' — you'd have hung on a bit.'

She eyed him helplessly. What good would staying around do and how could she explain to him that the longer she stayed, the harder it was for her to leave? They'd had their ups and downs but the feelings she had for him now would only flourish, despite her efforts to stop them, if she didn't get away.

'I have career problems to sort out; I told you, remember?' she said unsteadily. 'And there's nothing for me here.'

The words sounded stark and cruel, yet they were true. There *was* nothing for her here; nothing she had a right to. His expression hardened, and he turned away from her, not speaking for a moment.

'Then what's keeping you?' he asked in a muffled voice.

She had deserved the remark, she knew. Yet still it was like a slap in the face and she was unprepared for it. Her face whitened, and she turned, hurrying back the way she had come.

'Miss Forrester.'

Her intentions of reaching the Lodge

quickly were frustrated by the sound of someone calling her name. Turning reluctantly, she saw Joe Traynor eyeing her hesitantly.

'Hello, Joe.' Despite her impatience to be away from the scene, she spoke patiently, waiting until the old man caught up with her. 'I'll be leaving soon, by the way,' she told him as he reached her side.

'We hoped you'd stay.' He spoke gruffly and there was a hint of reproach in his eyes. Far from angering her, it warmed Tansy's heart to hear it. He must think she belonged here, to say that . . . His expression was troubled and he seemd at a loss for words, now that he had her attention.

'What is it, Joe?' She eyed him in concern. 'Is there something wrong?'

He hesitated, and a thought suddenly occurred to her.

'You know your cottages are safe, don't you?' she asked, feeling this was the reason for the anxiety she saw now in his face. 'Mark — Mr Harmon

— will have told you I'm not selling to Tregarth after all.'

'It's not that, though we do thank you for it,' he muttered. 'The thing is, I've something troubling my conscience, miss, and I know it's my duty to tell someone. But I can't talk to Mr Harmon about it; being as how he's so friendly with Miss Parker, like . . . '

'What are you trying to tell me, Joe?' Tansy eyed him frowningly, her interest aroused by his mention of Mark and Heather.

'Well, miss — ' He hesitated, then seemed to make up his mind. 'I don't want to go getting anyone in trouble, but I have to unburden myself. I can't keep it to myself any longer.'

'Keep what to yourself?' Anxiety sharpened Tansy's voice. 'Come on, Joe. Tell me what's bothering you that you can't talk to Mr Harmon about.' She eyed him encouragingly.

'Well, 'twere last night before the fire, see.' He spoke slowly, still reluctant to divulge the thing which was troubling him. 'I was in the greenhouse here, and I saw someone going into the meadow. I thought nothing of it at first, then all of a sudden, there was the fire and it was only later that I started to ponder on things.'

Tansy drew in her breath. 'You saw someone going into the meadow just before the fire started?' She spoke tensely. 'You think it might have been the person who — ' She broke off at the anguished expression on his face. 'Who was it, Joe?' she asked urgently. 'Who did you see going into the meadow?'

'Miss Heather, it was,' he said haltingly. 'She seemed upset like, then moments later I saw the flames.'

Tansy felt herself go cold with shock, as she realized what the old man was telling her . . .

7

'It was Heather you saw going into the meadow?' Tansy caught at the old man's arm. 'You're sure, Joe?'

He nodded, fidgeting unhappily with his cap. 'I had to tell someone,' he muttered. 'I couldn't keep quiet; not about a thing like that.'

Tansy pushed a distracted hand through her hair, hoping desperately that he would clarify his words with some kind of explanation, yet he remainded silent now. Gazing helplessly at him, she noted his distress. He had been at the nurseries since he was a boy, had probably worked closely with Heather for years, and it had obviously taken a great effort for him to report what he had seen, the way he had. She could only guess at the strain he had been under since the previous day. Surely there had to be some other explanation for what he had seen? Heather had rushed off in an agitated state, after overhearing Tansy telling Mark she was her half-sister. What was more natural than that she would head for the meadow, a place she loved and took great pride in, which at the same time gave her the privacy she needed, to cope with the emotions Tansy's revelations had aroused in her? It had to be a coincidence! Yet, if she had been in the meadow just before the fire and had not been responsible for it herself, surely she must have seen whoever had been responsible? So far as Tansy knew, Heather had said nothing about being there herself or seeing anyone else there, a fact which only served to make her guilt more probable. Why would she do such a terrible thing — if she *had* done it? Benson Whitton and she had planted the meadow together; why would she want to destroy it? Even as she asked herself that question, a possible answer was slipping into Tansy's mind. Already overwrought at

Tansy's disclosures about her background, had Heather's anger turned in on the man who had allowed her to believe she was a blood relative all her life, going momentarily beyond her control so that she wanted to strike out at him? The meadow had been his pride and joy; those had been Heather's own words, Tansy recalled. In destroying it, she would, in a certain frame of mind, feel she was hitting back at him in the only way left open to her. Was that how it happened? Tansy shook her head wretchedly. Surely not? To destroy something so beautiful . . . Yet she'd had no difficulty in thinking Paul Tregarth capable of it, not so long ago. What was so different about Heather doing it, for reasons far stronger than Tregarth's more mercenary ones? She refused to allow herself to believe it. Heather wasn't ruthless and cold-blooded like Tregarth; she was a woman with emotions and feelings. Wasn't it all the more logical then, an inward voice asked, that she would have given in to an impulsive, violent gesture such as setting fire to the meadow?

Feeling sick at heart, Tansy looked at the old man. He was regarding her with an expression of mingled sympathy and relief now; sympathy for the dilemma with which he had burdened her; relief that it was no longer his responsibility.

'Don't mention this to anyone else,' she told him then. 'I'll deal with it.'

'You can rely on me, miss.'

He moved away, leaving Tansy to wrestle with the turmoil his revelations had aroused in her. What was she to do, she thought helplessly? If she told Mark, it was possible he wouldn't believe her. And if he did, he would insist on tackling Heather about it. Nor would he thank Tansy for telling him, she knew that instinctively. Heather and he were close; any suggestion that she was responsible for the fire which had destroyed the meadow could shatter him. And yet, the only other alternative was to say nothing.

Tansy continued on her way, her

mind preoccupied now with the implications of what Joe Traynor had told her. There might well be an innocent explanation for Heather's presence in the meadow, but whatever the reason, it was something Tansy would keep to herself, she decided now. Heather was her half-sister, the child Tansy's father had abandoned. If she had, for a few seconds, allowed her emotions to override her judgement, forcing her to seek revenge in an act of uncontrollable anger, then it was Tansy's fault as much as anyone's. If Heather had not learned of her real parentage so brutally from Tansy, she would not have reacted as she had. She would never know from Tansy that she had been seen going into the meadow. It would be a secret she would take away from the island with her . . .

Conversation was superficial at lunch. She had accepted Laura's invitation to eat with them, not wanting to be alone in the gloomy Lodge, yet the strained atmosphere had Tansy wishing the meal would soon be over. Mark had seemed preoccupied; now he put down his knife and fork and sat back in his chair, appearing to come to a decision.

'I didn't know whether to mention it or not — ' He looked at Tansy. 'I had a call from that supermarket chain this morning.'

'Oh?' She eyed him questioningly.

He sighed then. 'I told you we hadn't heard the last of Tregarth.' His eyes smouldered. 'That deal we fixed to supply them with plants is off. They're not going ahead.'

'Oh, Mark!' Tansy eyed him in consternation. 'But I thought it was all settled — '

'So did I,' he interrupted bitterly. 'The legal people were drawing up the contracts. All that was needed were our signatures.'

'Then why?' Tansy eyed him blankly.

'Officially?' He shrugged. 'Financial cutbacks. Unofficially?' His mouth twisted. 'Well, I happen to know that Tregarth has some influence in that direction. He's friendly with one or two of the directors, I hear.'

'But surely he can't — '

'Can't he?' There was a cynical note in Mark's voice as he interrupted her. 'It won't be the first time he's lost us business and I dare say it won't be the last.'

'Surely we can do something about it?' Tansy asked pensively.

'Not much, at this stage,' he responded. 'But we managed before we got that contract. We've never let Tregarth get the upper hand before, and we won't now.'

Tansy seethed with indignation. Despite Mark's philosophical attitude, she knew how jubilant he had been about winning that contract and the injustice of it burned in her. Yet there was something in what he said. Tregarth did not have influence in every quarter; there would be other contracts. Sooner or later, he would have to accept the fact that he was wasting his time and that his bullying tactics would not pay off. But, coming on top of the fire, the loss of the contract was a blow . . .

'Heather's taking a day or two's leave,' Mark said then, changing the subject.

'In order to avoid me?' Tansy's tone was wry. 'There was no need; I won't go chasing after her. If she wants to talk, she knows where I am.'

Yet she felt deflated, in spite of her determined words. It would be sad if, having found her half-sister, Heather did not want to acknowledge the relationship. She could understand her feelings, and only hoped the other woman would come to feel differently, given time.

After lunch, she went for a walk, aware that this would be her last chance to see the island. Reaching the point where the road swooped upwards through woodlands, her eyes went to the spot where Merlin's Cavern was situated. From this distance she could not see it, yet her mind had no difficulty going back to the time when

Mark had taken her up there. It seemed so long ago now, so many things had happened since then, yet the peace she had felt in that enchanted spot remained sharply etched in her memory. It was a peace which eluded her now ... Turning, she made her way back towards the Lodge. There was someone lingering by the gate, and Tansy's heart lifted as she recognized Heather's slight figure. Quickening her steps, she approached the other woman, smiling tentatively.

'Heather! I'm glad to see you!'

'Can we talk?' Heather eyed her hesitantly

'Of course! Come in — '

'No; let's just walk down the lane a little,' Heather suggested.

'Whatever you like.' Falling into step with her, Tansy ventured a cautious glance at the other woman. She was pale, her eyes showing signs of constant weeping, and Tansy sighed, knowing she was the cause of Heather's misery. Obviously unsure of herself, Heather seemed at a loss for words and wisely Tansy waited for her to regain her composure.

'I've decided to leave Calanara,' Heather said at last.

'Leave?' Tansy eyed her in bewilderment. 'But — '

'I've been thinking about it for some time,' Heather hastened to assure her. 'I've had a couple of offers — one of them from my old college — recently, and I was tempted. I've always wanted to branch out into horticultural research and — well, this is as good a time as any.'

'Does Mark know what you've decided?' Tansy asked.

Heather shook her head. 'I'll be going to see him shortly.'

'It's not because of me?' Tansy caught at her arm. 'I never wanted that.'

'No; my reasons are — ' To Tansy's horror, Heather's face crumpled and she broke into tears. Instinctively Tansy stopped walking, putting her arms around the other woman.

'It was my fault.' It was an agonized whisper when Heather managed to speak again. 'The meadow; I did it — I set fire to it . . . '

'Don't talk about it yet,' Tansy urged gently. 'I know, anyway.'

'You know?' Heather eyed her through her tears. 'How?'

'It doesn't matter,' Tansy murmured. 'But don't worry. Mark doesn't know.'

'I have to tell him,' Heather insisted.

'Why?' Tansy urged. 'There's no reason he should ever know . . . '

'Yes, there is.' Heather was gaining control of herself now, her voice shaky but firm. She eyed Tansy wonderingly then. 'Aren't you angry, knowing it was my fault?'

Tansy shook her head.

'I suppose it was because of what you found out — what you heard me saying to Mark?'

Heather gestured helplessly. 'I hated Benson for a while then,' she said unsteadily. 'He allowed me to believe I was a Whitton all these years. He should have told me; someone should have.' Her mouth trembled.

Holding her, Tansy felt a lump rising in her throat, and her arm tightened around the other woman.

'I'd have given anything for you not to have found out that way,' she said at last, her own voice shaking. 'But I wanted so much to find you, Heather.'

'Finding out the way I did doesn't excuse what I did,' Heather insisted. 'I just wanted to pay him back the only way I could.' Her eyes filled again with tears. 'I destroyed it, that beautiful meadow, just because I couldn't cope with the fact that I wasn't who I thought I was. I behaved like a criminal — '

'No!' Tansy spoke urgently. 'You were upset, Heather. It must have been a great shock, finding out about your parents like that. It was enough to make anyone do something they would regret later.'

'I tried to put it out, I really did!' Heather spoke despairingly. 'As soon as

I saw the flames, I realized what a wicked thing I was doing! But they had got a hold, Tansy; I couldn't put them out! I panicked then, and ran off for help. But it was too late, and later I couldn't bear anyone to know it was my fault!'

'No one will know,' Tansy comforted her. 'At least only two people. And we'll never speak of it, I can promise you.'

She smiled encouragingly at Heather and after a moment, Heather smiled back through her tears. Tansy was aware then of a feeling of thankfulness overwhelming her. Somehow, in the last few moments, she and Heather had stepped over the barriers of constraint, made a tacit pact that the bitterness and mistakes of the past should be forgotten. She felt closer to Heather then than at any time since coming to the island. They were almost strangers, yet they were sisters . . .

'Heather — ' She spoke painfully then. 'Must you go away? We've only just found each other.'

'I have to, don't you see that?' Heather eyed her appealingly. 'I need time. I can't stay here.'

She was right, Tansy acknowledged. For her own sake, she had to leave Calanara. She touched Heather's arm briefly.

'When you come back, the meadow will be in bloom again,' she told her. 'Mark will see to that.'

'I never really felt as if I belonged here, you know.' Heather spoke wistfully now. 'I only came back after college because of Benson. And Mark, of course. But I've known for a long time that Mark doesn't feel for me what I feel for him, and never will. It's best for both of us that I go. Perhaps I'll find someone on the mainland who'll love me as I need to be loved.' She eyed Tansy. 'The way Mark loves you . . . '

'What Mark feels for me isn't love,' Tansy broke in, laughing shakily. 'If that's why you feel you have to go, forget it! He's made his opinion of me clear enough. Even now, he only tolerates me because I'm what he calls 'the boss'.'

'You're wrong!' Heather insisted. 'He's pigheaded and proud, and it goes against the grain, his falling in love with the boss lady! Give him time to climb down from his lofty perch and come to terms with his feelings, Tansy.'

Tansy shook her head. 'I can't believe it.' She eyed the other woman helplessly. 'You're wrong about that.'

Heather looked down. 'I've known Mark for a long time and I'm telling you that you're more important to him than you think,' she murmured. 'And if I can't have him, I can't think of anyone I'd like to see him with more.' She made a determined effort at briskness then. 'I'd better get down there and tell him the whole thing, before I lose my courage.'

'You don't have to!' Tansy caught at her arm, but the other woman shook her off gently.

'Yes, I do,' she said quietly.

Turning, she walked quickly away

before Tansy could say anything else.

She watched her go, and when she turned to retrace her steps to the Lodge, her own face was tear-streaked. It seemed to her then that she had brought nothing but trouble to the people here on the island. The sooner she left, the better.

She eyed Mark tentatively that evening. Laura had insisted that she dine with them on this, her last evening on Calanara.

'I spoke to Heather earlier. She was on her way down to see you.'

He nodded. 'I'm not surprised she wants to leave the island,' he commented. 'I've sensed a restlessness in her for quite a while now, and yesterday's events just brought it to the boil. So if you're still blaming yourself, forget it. Leaving Calanara is the best thing Heather could do. If anything, finding out she wasn't a Whitton after all has set her free to live her own life.'

Tansy was silent, wondering if he really believed that, or if he were trying to make her feel better about the part she had unwittingly played in Heather's decision to leave.

'Nevertheless, I feel as if I'm driving her away,' she said at last.

'That's nonsense!' he protested. 'Heather's wasted here; she's quite brilliant, you know. She'll go far, once she's away from here.'

'But who'll help you re-plant the meadow?' Tansy asked. 'You *are* planning to re-plant it, aren't you?'

'We'll re-plant it, I assure you,' he told her. 'It's not that difficult. We have enough competent people around here to deal with it. And it's only partly destroyed, don't forget.'

Tansy eyed him thoughtfully then. Had Heather told him she was responsible for the fire, as she had said she would? She had been expecting him to broach the matter, but it was looking unlikely that he would. And why should he? Why betray Heather, a longstanding colleague and friend, to someone who was almost a stranger? It was natural that he would try to protect Heather, afraid that Tansy, as the owner of the nurseries, would take action against her, perhaps, if he told her the truth. It was a criminal act Heather had committed, after all, despite the fact that it had not been premeditated. She was aware again of the loyalty these people showed to each other, and with it came a feeling of sadness that the loyalty did not extend to her. She was Benson Whitton's granddaughter, after all, the owner of Whitton Lodge Nurseries, yet she was as much an outsider as ever, it seemed. She should have been told the truth of what had happened to the meadow and it was Mark's duty to tell her. It seemed that his thoughts were running along the same lines, because he eyed her pensively, then turned away so that she could not see his face.

'I've solved the mystery of who fired the meadow,' he said, over his shoulder. 'Heather told me what happened. It seems she went down there, to be alone for a while, after overhearing us talking. She lit a cigarette and, being so upset, carelessly didn't make sure the match was completely out before dropping it. She forgot about it, only realizing later that it must have been her match which had started the fire off.'

Tansy eyed his back silently. So that was the way it was going to be told — and she couldn't help a feeling of thankfulness. Mark would not betray Heather to her and she would never let him know that she knew the real story, for then she would have had to involve Joe, who had spoken to her in confidence, and so it would go on and on . . . Far better to bury the truth this time. Her grandfather had done that and it had caused havoc years later. Yet this was different; bringing out the facts would only hurt people again, and there had been enough of that on the island. Aware of the fact that Mark expected some reaction on her part, she sighed.

'Well, that's only what we thought; that someone had been careless. And worrying about the cause doesn't solve anything. We ought to be directing our thoughts towards how soon we can restore the meadow.'

'We?' He turned, his eyebrows arching. Now that the subject of Heather and the meadow had been dealt with, he seemed more relaxed. 'I thought you were going back on the morning ferry?'

'Yes, I am,' Tansy confirmed. 'I have to get back as soon as possible. You remember I told you there was a problem at the office?'

'Yes.' He eyed her thoughtfully. 'What are you going to do about it?'

'Well, I'm certainly not going to sit back and let it happen,' she said spiritedly. Her expression became grim as she recalled Mike Hollingworth's deviousness and David's betrayal.

'I didn't think you would,' Mark responded. 'And what if your boss refuses to back down — which seems likely, since he's gone as far as hinting to the most likely contender for the assignment that he's thinking of making changes?'

Tansy had no hesitation in replying. 'I'll be handing in my resignation,' she told him. 'So I'll be joining the ranks of the unemployed.' She smiled wryly. 'I'll be glad to leave, actually. Mike hasn't been the easiest of employers. And I should get another post easily enough.'

Mark didn't speak for a few moments, and when he did, his voice was carefully casual.

'If it's a challenge you're after, you could do worse than join us here. I can promise you it wouldn't be boring. Life is going to become pretty lively over the next few weeks, I imagine, now that Tregarth knows he's lost. I'll be fully occupied trying to anticipate his next move, besides running the nurseries. One thing I am sure of is that he won't meekly accept your decision not to sell. Another pair of hands would be an enormous help, particularly in view of Heather's departure.'

Tansy eyed him. 'You're offering me

a job as your assistant?' she asked, after a moment.

He had the grace to look embarrassed.

'Hardly,' he retorted. 'You are the owner, after all, until you decide otherwise. You have a good brain and your expertise would be invaluable. With you running the business side of things, I could concentrate on building up trade. In fact — ' He hesitated, then continued. 'I've been thinking for some time of trying to get a foothold in the mail order market, but haven't had the time to give to it. Now that the supermarket order's gone, we could try that area again. It would be hard going at first; we'd need to mount an intensive advertising campaign — but I don't need to tell you that. It's your job.' He looked at her. 'Interested?'

Tansy didn't immediately reply. His suggestion had taken her by surprise, after her earlier conviction that he wanted her to leave things completely in his hands. And why did she feel differently about staying on the island now, when she had viewed the prospect so gloomily on her arrival? Mark's idea held exciting possibilities; the chance to build up an entirely new side of the business; something which would tax her skills to the full. Yet might she just be exchanging Mike Hollingworth's domination for Mark Harmon's? He had made it clear all along that he would not stand for interference in the running of things at the nurseries.

'We'd fight, Mark!' she said helplessly at last. 'We'd fight all the time.'

'Probably,' he agreed calmly. 'But as I said, life wouldn't be boring. And it could be an interesting venture for both of us, going in for a new side-line like this together. Think about it.'

Tansy looked away, not wanting to commit herself in any way. Her own response to the idea of staying here had taken her unawares, and she needed time to think.

'You needn't view it as a long-term thing,' he pointed out unexpectedly.

'More an extension of your stay, whilst you're looking round for a suitable job in your own line. You might find it interesting, learning about the horticultural trade. There's a lot more to it than growing plants.'

Tansy eyed him. He had made no further mention of his earlier proposal of forming a workers' co-operative; it had been left rather in the air, she recalled. Had he changed his mind about it or been unable to get enough support from the others? His commitment to the nurseries was total; she would have had to be blind not to have seen that. Leaving the business in the hands of its employees was something which appealed to her more and more, when viewed against selling to an outsider. It might not be so lucrative in financial terms for her, but it would bring about a conclusion satisfactory to everyone.

'What about that idea you mentioned of a workers' co-operative?' She eyed him hesitantly. 'Is that still in your mind?'

He took his time about replying. 'I still have enough trust in the logic of things to hope it won't be necessary,' he murmured at last.

Tansy frowned. What was that enigmatic statement supposed to mean? Did he still feel she could be persuaded to stay as owner of the place? Had she given that impression recently? Things had relaxed so much between them lately that it was difficult to recall just what had been said. In any case, she was in no hurry to sell any longer; if the employees could come up with something, she was prepared to wait.

'I have to go and sort things out, Mark!' she said. 'And I need time to think. But if I did decide to come back for a while as you suggest, I would want as free a hand in running my side of things as you have.'

'Naturally.' He eyed her gravely. 'Does that mean you accept?'

'I didn't say that,' she hastened to tell him. 'All I meant was — '

'I know what you meant,' he

interrupted. 'And I wouldn't have expected anything else — not from Benson Whitton's granddaughter.'

There wasn't, Tansy acknowledged, an answer to that . . .

The evening passed quickly. She had accepted Laura's invitation to spend her last night at Gatehouse Cottage. There was not much packing to do; she had, she recalled, only expected to be here for a day or two. How long had she been here, in fact? It seemed like a lifetime. The hustle and bustle of the city was not something she looked forward to returning to, and it was a thought which surprised her. She had always seen the frantic pace and competition as something of a challenge. At least, if she never came here again, Calanara had taught her that, she thought, staring out of her bedroom window at the moonlit scene below. There was a peace here, a serenity which, though completely at variance with her usual lifestyle, had stirred something within her. If she hadn't come here, would she have learned to care about the things of nature the way she did now? Would an enchanted legend concerning a small wild flower have made the impression it had on her, if she had heard it in the city? She doubted if the legend would have survived, away from the island. It would have been crushed, trampled underfoot long ago by people who had no time to spare for such things. Only here, on Calanara, would it have retained its magic . . . There was a slight tap at the door, followed by Laura's voice.

'Come in, Laura.' Smiling, she moved away from the window, as the older woman came into the room. Wearing a dressing-gown and obviously ready to retire herself, she carried a tray with a steaming mug on it.

'I thought you might like some cocoa,' she murmured. 'It's my last chance to spoil you.'

'Thank you. I'd love some.' Tansy took the mug gratefully.

Perching on the end of the bed,

Laura regarded her pensively.

'It gives me a chance to say goodbye, too,' she said gently. 'We've so loved having you among us.'

It wasn't just polite talk. Tansy knew that Laura meant it. Leaning across, she touched the older woman's arm briefly.

'I've enjoyed my stay, too, despite the bad start we got off to,' she murmured. 'I just wish — ' She hesitated. ' — well, that Heather wasn't leaving. I can't help feeling that if I hadn't come, things would have gone on in the same way.'

'Perhaps they would, but it would have been the same in the end,' Laura responded. 'Mark would not have married her. At least now she has a chance to find the right person for her; Mark was never that.'

'Aren't you disappointed?' Tansy eyed her curiously. 'Heather would have made a perfect daughter-in-law.'

'Things have a way of working out.' Laura smiled.

Tansy had a feeling the older woman

was trying to tell her something, without actually stating it and it didn't take much to realize what that was . . . if only things could turn out the way people wanted them to! She eyed the other woman tentatively.

'Mark put forward a proposal for me to stay on a while at the nurseries. He plans to go into the mail order side of things and thought I could get it off the ground.' She eyed Laura tentatively. 'I'm not sure what I want to do — '

Laura didn't reply for a moment. 'He must want you to stay very badly for him to have suggested that,' she said at last. 'He's always liked to run things on his own. It will be good for him, having a business partner.'

'I haven't said I'd take it on yet,' Tansy said quickly.

Laura's only reply was a gentle smile . . .

It was hard, saying goodbye the following morning. She had made a quick trip down to the greenhouse to make her farewells to the staff and now it was time to leave for the ferry. Whitton Lodge was already locked up again, the key handed over into Laura's care.

'Well, Laura . . . ' Tansy took the older woman's hands in hers. 'It's time to say goodbye.'

'Au revoir,' Laura corrected. 'I'll keep things tidy at the Lodge for you.'

Tansy nodded, a lump rising in her throat. Laura was convinced she would return and she made no move to contradict her. Quickly she walked towards the door. Mark was driving her to the ferry terminal. Heather was leaving on the same boat, and would be travelling in with her parents.

The island was at its prettiest as they drove through the countryside, and Tansy looked round her wistfully. Caught by a sudden thought, she turned to Mark,

'I hope you haven't, in your plans for establishing the mail order side of the nurseries, any thoughts about trying to cultivate Merlin's Tears?' she asked. 'It would be a mistake, Mark.'

'It's been tried before without success,' he responded. 'The old man has made it obvious the flowers are only meant for us.'

Tansy eyed him thoughtfully. 'Despite your cynicism about all that. I can't help thinking you don't completely discount it as just folklore,' she murmured.

'I have to believe it; I'm an islander,' he said lightly. 'It's only outsiders, people from the city, who laugh at our stories.'

'Like me?' Tansy murmured, giving him a sidelong glance.

For a moment he didn't reply. 'You have the island's blood in your veins, whether you like it or not,' he said at last. 'You're leaving now, but you'll come back. And when you do, it won't be because of some misguided feeling of duty; it will be because you want to.'

Tansy looked away. Put like that, it seemed her future was already decided . . .

The Parkers were the first people she saw when they arrived at the ferry terminal. Catching Tansy's eye, Mrs Parker turned and walked quickly away, making it obvious that she had no wish to speak to her. Shrugging, Tansy let the matter rest. The woman's resentment had burned for a long time; there would be no quick forgiveness there for her.

'Hello.' Heather's smile seemed strained as they reached her side. 'Looks like it will be a smooth crossing.'

'Is your interview today?' Tansy asked.

'I have one at my old college today, and another at a research institute tomorrow,' Heather told her.

'Take care of yourself over there,' Harold Parker admonished, eyeing her in concern. 'Perhaps Miss Forrester will keep an eye on you.'

'I'm not a child, Dad!' Heather protested.

The way she addressed him so naturally as her father reassured Tansy that she hadn't done as much harm as she had feared . . . A thought suddenly occurred to her.

'You could stay with me if you haven't made any arrangements already,' she said tentatively. 'I live quite near the college, if you remember, and there's plenty of room.'

Heather hesitated.

'It sounds like a good idea,' Mark said unexpectedly. 'Why don't you do that, Heather?'

Tansy was aware of a feeling of gratitude towards him. He knew how much Heather's friendship meant to her.

'Well, if you're sure I won't be a bother?' Heather eyed Tansy hesitantly.

'You wouldn't be!' Tansy said quickly. 'It would be a pleasure for me to have your company.'

A warm feeling was spreading through her at the thought that she and Heather would not be losing contact, once away from the island. And they needed to be away from it, she realized; away from old memories and associations. On the mainland, with all that behind them, they would be able to meet each other on equal terms, get to know each other without the shadow of the past hanging over them.

She moved away then, in order to allow Mark to make his farewells to Heather. Stopping a few yards away, she waited as they spoke quietly to each other for a few moments. Then she saw Mark reach out and touch Heather's arm in a brief, conciliatory gesture. She had wondered how he felt about the fact that someone so close to him had been responsible for the partial destruction of something as precious to him as the meadow, and the poignancy of his gesture brought a sudden lump to her throat. It would have been so easy for him to turn against Heather, and in all fairness, she would not have been able to blame him. More than anything, she wanted Mark and Heather to remain friends. She couldn't help wondering then at the way things had turned out. She and Heather seemed to have changed places and, noting the anticipation on the other woman's face now as she looked out across the water towards the mainland, Tansy knew it was right for her to leave. All she was aware of, so far as she herself was concerned, was a sinking feeling at the thought of going back. She was a fool, she realized then. She wanted to stay; wanted to meet the challenge Mark Harmon had dangled before her of starting up the mail order side of the nurseries. What was there for her on the mainland? David, who had put ambition before friendship? A job where she was never likely to receive credit for good work, however hard she tried? A lonely flat and the prospect of finding herself another job? Here on Calanara, she would have a job and loyal friends. And then there was the main reason for that feeling which was invading her now; she did not want to leave Mark. There had been hostility between them at the start, thawing gradually to tolerance. Now they had the beginnings of a friendship based on mutual respect. There were no promises for the future, no guarantee that he would come to return the feelings she had been aware of growing within her for him; feelings which could only develop further, now she knew that he and Heather were not, and never had been, anything more than friends. He was back at her side now, as people began to board the ferry.

'Well, Tansy.' He eyed her enquiringly. 'Will we be seeing you again soon, do you think?'

She could have satisfied him with an inconsequential reply, a vague promise to return at some point, yet in the last few minutes she had surrendered to the decision which would change the course of her life, and it suddenly mattered to her that he knew of it.

'I thought I'd pop back here at the week-end, once I've sorted things out at the office.' She spoke unsteadily. 'I'll bring some advertising campaign literature with me. I thought we could go over things, make some tentative plans — '

He stared at her for a moment. People jostled them, and the ferry's blast sounded incongruously on the morning air. As Tansy turned anxiously towards the gangway, Mark caught at her arm, finding his voice at last.

'I'll be waiting,' he said.

We do hope that you have enjoyed reading this large print book.

Did you know that all of our titles are available for purchase?

We publish a wide range of high quality large print books including:
Romances, Mysteries, Classics
General Fiction
Non Fiction and Westerns

Special interest titles available in large print are:
The Little Oxford Dictionary
Music Book, Song Book
Hymn Book, Service Book

Also available from us courtesy of Oxford University Press:
Young Readers' Dictionary
(large print edition)
Young Readers' Thesaurus
(large print edition)

For further information or a free brochure, please contact us at:
Ulverscroft Large Print Books Ltd.,
The Green, Bradgate Road, Anstey,
Leicester, LE7 7FU, England.
Tel: (00 44) **0116 236 4325**
Fax: (00 44) **0116 234 0205**

JUST A SUMMER ROMANCE

Karen Abbott

When Lysette Dupont decides to help her grandfather restore his old windmill on Ile d'Oléron off the west coast of France, she doesn't want to get sidetracked into pursuing a deepening interest in the bohemian artist Xavier Monsigny. Xavier has planned to spend his time on the island painting and sketching — but intrigue and danger draw them into a summer romance . . . for, surely, that is all it will be?

A FAMILY SECRET

Jo James

Symons Hill is a charming, close-knit Australian town, where April Stewart's happiness is linked to Symon Andrews of the area's pioneering family. When he leaves suddenly for the city, rumours abound. Heartbroken, April immerses herself in her animal refuge work until he returns unexpectedly. Though he reawakens her feelings, his actions threaten to change the relaxed character of Symons Hill. What has happened to change this once warm, thoughtful man, and how will April learn the truth?

BECAUSE OF YOU

Catherine Brent

Kay Ballard, a primary school teacher, obtained a position as companion to the children of Simon Nash, the composer ... But at Ashleigh, Kay discovered that the composer's home and background were surrounded by mystery. Three years earlier Simon Nash's wife had died in peculiar circumstances, out of which rumour had sprung and flourished ... How much of the rumour was false, and how much based on fact, became an obsession with Kay. And when the mystery was explained, danger and tragedy were in the air once more.

STAR ATTRACTION

Angela Dracup

To be on tour with Leon Ferrar should be a dream come true, but for Suzy Grey, his assistant, it becomes a nightmare when she finds herself in love with him. Leon is surrounded by beautiful women, from the voluptuous Toni Wells to pianist Angelina Frascana. Leon and Angelina draw close together as they prepare for a concert in Vienna, but Suzy's desperate course of action threatens to ruin her own relationship with Leon for ever.

GLENALLYN'S BRIDE

Mary Cummins

Queen Johanna destroyed the House of Frazer at Dundallon, after the murder of James I. Innes Frazer, step-sister to Sir Archibald, escaped but was captured by a band of beggars. The leader of the beggars, Ruari Stewart, offers her as a bride to Glenallyn. Innes refuses, only to become a servant of the Queen at Edinburgh Castle, where she again meets James Livingstone who was responsible for slaughtering the Frazers. Innes knows that she must find Ruari Stewart, and one day she might become Glenallyn's bride.